Apples

Richard Milward

faber and faber

First published in 2007
by Faber and Faber Limited
3 Queen Square London WC1N 3AU

Typeset by Faber and Faber
Printed in England by Mackays of Chatham, plc

The right of Richard Milward to be identified as author of this work
has been asserted in accordance with Section 77 of the Copyright,
Designs and Patents Act 1988

A CIP record for this book
is available from the British Library

ISBN 978-0-571-23282-6

4 6 8 10 9 7 5 3

APPLES

Thank You

Francis Bickmore + Canongate, Lee Brackstone + Faber, Pia Conaghan, Emily Dewhurst, family, Matthew Firth + *Front&Centre*, friends, Vinita Joshi + Rocket Girl, Cathryn Summerhayes + DGA, Emma Warren + *The Face*. And you.

Contents

Chapter One

She Is Sick

Eve

We got a McDonald's the night my mam got lung cancer. Jenni was sat there smoking a superking, and I was trying not to sit there so upset. We looked weird dressed up and stuffing our faces, but I couldn't eat a thing. I was hungry though. I didn't have the heart to ask Mam for money, so I had to excavate a tenner out of my piggy-bank and hope to god it got me pissed. I slumped back in the plastic seat, watching Rachel squirt sauce on her chips while she messed around with her mobile. She was probably getting harassed by one of the boys she was screwing, but no wonder – Rachel had Hollywood hair and her skin was gold and rainbowed, but she reckoned she didn't want a boyfriend or any of that massive commitment right now. When I broke up with Fairhurst I was glad to see the back of all boys, but when you're out of a relationship you want to be in one and when you're in a relationship you want to be out. Actually I broke with Fairhurst after he felt Rachel's tit at a party, and I doubted she'd last a week without getting up to something naughty. But you're only young the once.

What's wrong? Gracie asked – she always asked crap boring questions. I shrugged her eyes off, then we watched a smackhead causing trouble at the counter, and tried not to laugh while he kicked off at the moron serving. I was flickering between happy and sad, and it annoyed me. Sometimes it's good to talk about stuff, but I couldn't tell the girls about Mam – I'd only known about it myself a couple of hours, and they didn't want some blonde bimbo putting a big downer on the night. The plan was just to get drunk and block it out, but there we were sat in the depressing white light at Ronald's. It spun a shiver in the threads of my dress – Mam sat me and my sisters down in the living room, and you could see it was bad news. She had that serious tone of voice, and watery eyes. I was cross-legged on the carpet watching kids' telly and thinking up dresses and make-up, then all of a sudden my mam was dying. But it wasn't like me to be always looking on the down side, and Mam thought she might be okay and we had a bear hug and a little cry. I still wanted to go out and see my friends.

Jenni bit into her McChicken sandwich, and I laughed inside because at school they reckon the boys at McDonald's spunk in them. I started to lose my appetite, and it was very welcome. You wouldn't even really want your own boyfriend's stuff in your mouth. I got back so late from school (me and Dan read the magazines at Bells, he stole us some Anglo Bubbly and we blew it up together on the courtyard), I only managed a couple of custard creams for tea and my insides felt like a cave. I glanced back at the smack-head trying to score a free Happy Meal or something, and I thought to myself if they could afford all that horrid smack how couldn't they stretch to some burgers and fries? But then I thought about us swallowing ecstasy pills together, and not giving one hoot about eating or sleeping or weeing or any other bodily functions. Perhaps he was going cold turkey, his hunger coming back with a vengeance dead unexpected. The boys behind the counter were clearly panicking, but they tried to look cool in the baseball caps and I wouldn't put it past Jenni to suck their dicks anyway. I smiled the Urban Decay right across my face. That's a lipstick.

Are you not eating, Eve? Rachel asked me, picking bits out of her burger. You can have that minging gherkin, if you want.

We laughed, but in the end I stole some chips off her. I gobbled them down, then ducked my eyes and murmured, I'm so skint. Just gonna save my money til we get in Empire.

I couldn't wait to get in the club – it'd been a hard week, what with the exams and the cancer and everything. I promise you now I wasn't intending on dwelling on it, it's just the sitting around doing nothing that was getting to me. We needed to move! Kicking all the thoughts from my head, I tugged blonde fringe out my eyes then clippety-clopped my high-heels on the dirty floor. The empty stomach would at least get me dead hammered.

I bet some handsome stranger buys you loads of drinks ... anyway, look you could even work here if you wanted. Debbie pointed at the poster STAFF REQUIRED, and I was surprised she could read it because she was always banging on about her dyslexia. It's true that thing about dyslexics being good artists – I taxed another chip off Rachel's tray, then stared as Debbie scrawled a cartoon girl on the tabletop. She squeaked the Magic Marker in between stains and rubbish, tracing a black babe with big boobies and seventies Afro. She had on typical star-shape sunglasses, and the shading was all cross-hatched and professional. Debbie wasn't black, but she signed her tag everywhere like a nigger and she only ever went out with black boys or half-castes. It was funny the way she spelled her name DEBE like she was putting on the disease, but the letters were always mad and funky and we buzzed off her. I didn't know why she always came out with a marker, though.

Debbie coughed and scratched her dark braids, each one of them perfect but you could tell she was bored as me. Jenni was finishing that nasty cigarette, and she stubbed it on the brown tray, probably melting it but I didn't care to look. This was my mam's outlook on getting wrecked: drink as much as you want and bring home boys now and again, just never ever smoke a cigarette. Health-wise I think it's even worse than taking pills and whatnot, and I didn't like the taste anyhow. It's nicer taking something to make you happy than make you completely reek. I adjusted the blue-silver top, watching people come and go over Jenni's shoulder while Rachel kept beeping her phone next to me. I wondered what sick things she was getting sent. At school these girls from the richer estates had boyfriends who took them to smart restaurants before the Cornerhouse or Tall Trees or wherever – the most expensive place Fairhurst ever took me was G-Force down Linthorpe Road, for his alloy wheels. McDonald's was okay, but it seemed ever so lonely in the bright lights with only a little bit of movement outside and my girls not really talking to each other much. I wondered if we had more of a laugh at Brackenhoe than out on the town. I thought about Mam and I thought about

4

getting IDed at the theatre; my hollow belly was full of butterflies, and all they had was a couple of French fries to surf around on.

You spoke to Claire today? Rachel asked me, since I was in her Maths class on Fridays. She's not replying.

Rachel shoved her mobile back in the croc-print bag, then finished off the chips as I went, Yeah.

Is she coming out or not?

Naw, well isn't she grounded? I think she's having loads of hassle with Shane and all, I explained. I couldn't imagine staying at home knowing all the girls were out, but her step-dad was probably a bastard. I wasn't positive why she'd been grounded – often she made up excuses like that just so she could stay at home and shag her boyfriends. She was sort of the loose one. The daftest excuses so far had been debt, period pain, and petit mal epilepsy. She was a drama queen. I could see regular sex getting boring though, after all most of it's just laying there getting pounded, but everyone gets their kicks differently. Gracie was the only one I had doubts about – she might not've been a virgin, but she always dressed angelic and acted shy in front of boys. She had that sort of Drew Barrymore look; innocent and pretty, but from the wrong angle you could accuse her of being a mong. She tended to attract a load of nonces – in actual fact this group of oldish men were gazing at us across the white restaurant. We made plans to hit some bars pretty sharpish – no one was in the mood to get raped, and I was feeling fidgety. Dyslexic Debbie held the McDoor open for me and my friends, then we dashed into the night. I joined up with Jenni and we clattered up the pavement nice and quick – the streets looked shimmery and fantastic, and I hadn't even drunk anything. I smiled and hugged Jenni a little bit closer, then we set off on the rampage.

Adam

I had to shut the door seven times or else my family dies. I also had to put *With The Beatles* on a couple of times, only because it's a good one. I got transfixed by all the words, lying back in bed and smacking my head off the wood frame. Back then they were always crooning about courting girls and twisting and shouting and that, but all I ever did on the weekends was sit around in a shit mood. I stuck 'Don't Bother Me' on full-blast, though you could still hear my dad slamming the door on his way out. Every Friday he got lashed after work and went over the Beechwood Easterside Social, and I sat up and pondered if he'd left any drinks in his bedroom. I couldn't stand being a boring cunt. I watched out the window Dad walking along then crossing Deighton Road, the sun lounging in the background and whacking off the housetops. I had to shut the curtains six or seven times or else he'd get struck by lightning.

Two disc spins later I was still sat on my bed and my head was knacking from all the inaction. The Yellow Submarine clock only said 8:31, and I crept out of the room with white spots in my eyes. I let the guitars continue clanging off the walls and furniture, then snuck my head round the door and tried to keep my toes quiet. All the kids at school had started to boast about drinking and doing sexual intercourse, but the nearest I'd been was that brandy at Christmas and wetdreaming myself over the girl with the boobies at the end of *Magical Mystery Tour*. It took me about an hour to finish a little glassful, the brandy I mean, and I went around licking the walls and being off my head. The wet dream resulted in me changing my sheets for the first time.

I spun softly into my parents' room, over-exaggerating the detective footsteps – is it quieter walking on the balls of your feet or the heels? It was always frightening going in there – that one time I saw my mum getting changed was enough to scar me for life. She had yellow skin from smoking too much, and tits like potatoes. They hadn't even made the bed since this morning, and you could still sort of smell the smell. I fumbled round the diamond wallpaper but there was no really obvious place to hide a crate of lager, and I couldn't go down to the kitchen because Mum was there chaining the Mayfairs, and she'd fucking go mad at me. I stood around, then went for my dad's cabinet, where he kept important things like aftershave and creams and massive undies. It was a bit too cramped for a keg of beer, but there could've been a bottle of whisky rolling about. I ended up disappointed. I tried to make it look like I hadn't been snooping around, but it was difficult having to shut everything five or six times and I felt like I was being noisy.

'Adam, you got any washing?!' Mum screamed from downstairs. My heart jumped out of my jumper, and I scuttled from the drawers then yelled back, 'Naw.'

I thought for a second if I put my school uniform in the basket or not, but I wasn't bothered. I hated school. I got my breath back, put my hands on my hips, then went looking in the cupboards but I couldn't drink any of his shirts or overalls either. I was getting desperate, keeping my eyes peeled for bottletops or ring-pulls but there was nothing left to do really. I straightened the floral sheets. You could still hear the Beatles enjoying themselves in the room next door, and I thought what fucking knobhead couldn't even get merry on a Friday night. I daydreamed all the kids at school indulging in a massive multicolour orgy and me not invited. I was frustrated – I checked every one of my dad's socks for a can of Carling. His drawers were full of shit, and I leaned right into them, the lightbulb glinting off dingy polyester and money and the odd journal. Most of them were old Boro programmes, but delving in a bit deeper that was when I found the magazine called *Razzle*. It looked sick – the girl on the front was permed to the max, with her teeny tits popping out of this Day-Glo top or whatever it was. Later on in the book, she was naked and all bent over like she'd dropped something. I skimmed through it on my lap, chock-a-block with eighties girls in crap skirts and knickers, some of them getting off with each other but mostly just hanging out in their bedrooms. I didn't know whether to stiffen up or shrivel up – the fanny parts did look kind of mangled. Some were brown and dropping out, others were like pink seafood. I couldn't believe the girls at Brackenhoe were like that between the legs – I always imagined your minge to be a sort of innocent V-shape like how you draw them at school. The ones in *Razzle* were sewer rats. In the past I used to cut out girls' heads from magazines and pencil them in filthy poses, but I always did have artists' block when it came to the special little details. Waking up, I suddenly got very aware of perusing a porno in my parents' room, so I chucked it back in the drawer and limped out to the landing. I sat back on my bed and thought about what I'd learned. At 10:13 I put on the White Album, but I couldn't concentrate on the music with all those flowers in my head. I drifted in and out of a funny sleep. I wasn't even bothered about not drinking, my head was in a jumble anyway. When Disc One finished I had to shut the lid seven times or else the world would end. I didn't have to shut my eyes seven times; I was too tired. I dreamt of a day playing something like 'Happiness is a Warm Gun' or 'Helter Skelter' to a girl, but they probably wouldn't get it. I dreamt of a night with loads of mangled fannies instead.

Eve

The Hard made his willy soft. We stayed in bed til about eight or nine, our heads clanging like we had buckets on them. I put back on the CK knickers and went into the bathroom. You could tell he wanted me to come back to bed, but I was shattered and in the morning touching was always a bit sickly. My head was fried. I got myself freshened up, then he walked me to the bus-stop and I had to kiss him bye but I wasn't fussed if he phoned me. We had sweet breath like a dustbin lorry. The sex was okay, but you could tell we were wrecked because we couldn't get it in and he kept losing his erection and I woke up with a bit of a sore throat. He didn't appreciate the poppers.

I was pretty nervous about getting IDed in the Empire, but all you had to do was poke out your 32Cs and get through the doors. The excitement! It was still early and I was pissed offof the Reef and those shots bought for us in Bar Zantia. Gracie was tugging on my sparkly top as we queued up, and I felt seriously low on energy as I paid the girl with the sad face on the counter. I needed food, but instead we got Aftershocks at the bar since it was pretty empty. We got eyeballed by the packs of wolves, dumb

9

wankers – Gracie was lapping it up, but the boys were mostly losers and all they ever did was try and grapple you into bed. I liked it really, but we'd only just walked in the door and I didn't want a night of running away from stinkers. We had the shots then went for shelter in the ladies; Rachel gave her red cheerleader jacket to the cloakroom and the other girls waited about with her. We were a motley crew – I grimaced in the mirror, throwing a bit of powder on and the Urban Decay even though I didn't like using it up. You could see my eyes dropping – the adrenalin was going, but it was dead fake energy like popping a pill when you've got a cold. I picked out a bit of black sludge, then dragged Gracie outside again because there was no more time to mope around.

We dancing in a bit? Debbie shouted at me, and you had to because the house music was so loud. I nodded, a bit zombified, watching Rachel getting hitted on. I didn't realise she'd come out in the gold porno top, and I laughed to myself because she always took guys for a total ride. She ended up with two watermelon Breezers, then fucked off to the dancefloor with us lot. It was emptyish round the stage, but that's what you got for setting off too early – we'd only been to Zantia and the Ex, and in winter it feels a lot later than it really is. The love-heart on my arm said 10:16, and it seemed to be spinning slower than normal.

Bacardi Breezer Person tried to hang out with us for a couple of dances, swishing about Rachel like a floppy dick, then he got the hint and slinked off someplace else. In a way you felt bad about blowing men's wages, but at least they had the money and you weren't really forcing them. Rachel smiled an eensy bit, then went to me, Here have one of these. I know you're skint and that . . .

I didn't even like watermelons. I clenched the bottle, then spotted Dan Williams in the opposite corner and I had to go over. He was cute as anything in a new whitey shirt, and I tried to chat him up but he wasn't receptive to that sort of thing. Rachel liked him too, and I wondered how long her promise to stay off boys was going to last. She appeared at my elbow in two seconds flat. So we bantered for a while, not really knowing what each other was saying, and I couldn't really get rid of Rach because I was drinking her drink. Dan was sexy, but he also seemed to care about you and loads of times we walked home together and went on adventures. Over there, it looked like Jenni and the Dyslexic had got the hump and they stormed up the ledge to the bar, trailing Grace since she was easily taken into stuff. Debbie had this boyfriend from North Ormesby called Brandon (coloured, of course), but Jenni always got jealous of me and Rachel knocking around with stud-muffins. Jenni wasn't the prettiest bush in the garden; she tended to settle for absolute monsters or worm her way into mine and the girls' sexy rejects. The last lad she'd been with was a twenty-year-old care-worker with a hare lip.

I stammered around on the dancefloor, then erupted into full-blown dancing as the place filled up. The drinks were starting to feel quite whirly, and I managed to drag Rachel off Danny boy and get her for a boogie – she was just about to perk her tits up in the gold top. We kissed him goodbye very competitively.

Where are the others? Rachel yelped, getting about as excited as me as she finished off her Bacardi. I pointed to the balcony where those three were intentionally looking sour-faced, probably booing and hissing while we span each other round and round. But I didn't want them being sad on a Friday night. In the end I grabbed Rachel's hand and we had to go collect them – we were too mature for any stupid attitude like that. We fell up the stairs.

What youse doing?

Jenni just looked at me, but she was pleased we trekked up. I was blistering in new heels, but the girls were worth it. Jenni had an overbite and one boob bigger than the other, and I always figured that's why we fell out so much – sometimes it was over boys, sometimes it was over outfits and doing things at breaktimes, but she'd been jealous of me since Beechwood Juniors. I was sheer perfection. But it turned out the girls weren't even that cross with us – Jenni had poppers in her bag and they were all getting whacked-out while me and Rachel were dancing. I took it off them – me, Debbie and Brandon often had laughs in that sex shop down Boro, giggling at the horse sex and fetish videos then getting the Turkish guy to score us nitrate. He always had the real gayboy types like Hard and Liquid Gold, but that made it funnier and we tended to sniff them on the way back to Brandon's, him driving while me and Deb floated in zero gravity.

Woo, I said, getting a hot flush as the bottle kicked in. For a second I forgot we were in the Empire – everything got a bit vibrant and I laughed in the girls' faces. Before you knew it the rush was over, and I passed the poppers back to Jenni all shaky. We spent the next twenty minutes enjoying it Hard on the balcony, keeping very surreptitious sniffing it up. I got the bottle back from Rach, nearly dropping the dinky lid as I came up again. It was like a half-minute of joy and glazing over then back to normal. The third time, I couldn't stop touching the banister with the wood sensation going through me, and I knew I was staring into space with a dossed grin on my face but I was enjoying myself. We were killing ourselves. Then our heads started throbbing, and we decided to go downstairs to laugh at the lights. I ended up with the poppers in my handbag, weaving my way around all the lovely people.

Time felt like a rollercoaster, a really fun one. You could tell we were all yearning for the poppers again but me and my girls formed a circle somewhere on the stage, and we danced like angels coming down from heaven. If only we'd scored some ecstasy – poppers were amazing and disappointing. We were all up and down but it was so funny – Rach and Debbie stomped on needlepoints and Gracie nearly boinged out of the white dress. It was heating up, and I started to feel sweaty as loads of men gathered around again. Occasionally I said sorry when I bumped bums into someone else, but it always happened to be a horny lad who tried to grope me straight after. For a breather we kept going to the loo for more Hard, me and Debbie taking it up really fast then charging back to the dancefloor in the hope it lasted. All we ended up doing was smiling in everyone's way.

This is Ben; he used to babysit us, Gracie said to me when we got back. At first I thought she'd pulled the fine specimen – he was older than us, with a scruffy sort of haircut and a very nice jawline. He was quite the honeypot.

Hi, how's it going, I said, trying to play it cool but staying up close and personal so Rachel or Jenni couldn't get a look-in. They both had Bacardis (not sure if they were from

Breezer Person again), crushed in one spot surrounded by boys' heads. I stuck my dimples out, then accidentally-on-purpose touched Ben's sides and he was saying, Are you having a good night? You look dead familiar. Are you same age as Grace?

Nah, I'm like eighteen, I said, and I lied. It'd probably put him off if I seemed like a little baby, or maybe it'd turn him on but he didn't seem the type. I was only fifteen. He bared loads of teeth and told me he was twenty-two, which was partly scary but when we started dancing together I felt so grown-up. I didn't go in for the kill straight away – I kept a good distance from his lips even though our bodies were pushed right up, and I tried to feel for that thing in his jeans on my skirt but I couldn't tell. He was a good dancer – we had a laugh spinning each other about and being daft, and I was glad Gracie had the other girls to boogie with so she didn't feel isolated. I said something corny to Ben, then that thing happened where your faces hang for a bit in the air then drift together – it's called a kiss. And you could tell from the dancing and tonguing he'd be ace in the sack. I figured I'd take him back – the poppers told me that. He kept coming in and out for snogs, but I kept the secret to myself.

Ben's lips were strawberry bootlaces. I got the impression there hadn't been much action in Ben's life recently since he was so dirty with me, but he could've been wrecked and all that. Eventually he was quite the gentleman and got us both a drink. We squirmed through bodies bopping and I pecked my friend Ste's cheek, asking him how he was quickly before me and Ben made it to the bar. He was okay I think. In the queue Benjamin asked me where I lived and what I did – I mentioned something about Beechwood and the name of a college. He worked for some firm in Middlesbrough, and it sounded a bit shit but at least he'd have money and good prospects. I didn't even know what I wanted to do when I grew up – I did model for *Sugar* magazine once the year before, and I started to regret not saying I was a model. I tucked my fingers in his shirt and gazed at him buying us vodka and Cokes which came to about six pound. He was a keeper.

After the petrol Cokes I began to feel shit. All the colour fell off my face, and I didn't know if the tight feeling inside was lack of food or poppers but it was quite obvious I'd had too much bevvy. And once you think that, there's no going back. I tried my hardest to keep kissing Ben, feeling my tummy churn up all the shit and crap and my head felt like it was splitting. I couldn't carry on dancing – I was a wobbly mess. I forced one more peck on his lips, then chickened out and said, I'm just nipping to the loo.

Then I stormed quickly as I could to the bathroom, pushing through bunches of lasses and getting all the brutal looks off them. They were jealous little bitches, but I was in a desperate state of affairs. I almost cried as I locked myself in the white cubicle, then nervously retched a few times before sicking all over the toilet. It was brownish, and I wasn't sure why. I should've eaten something. I burped up a bit more spew, then tried to wipe off the rim and flush it. All my energy whirlpooled down the toilet, and all I wanted to do was fall asleep or pass out – I checked the love-heart and it said after one, but the girls always wanted to stay til three and I wasn't sure I could take it. I chucked the cover down and sat for a while, deep breathing and trying to stop my head spinning. I knew from experience not to shut your eyes – when we used to go to Millennium in about Year Nine, once upon a time we got the all-inclusive drinks and I got thrown out for throwing up and passing out on the sofas. I wondered for a second who had to clean up the sick after a night out. I sighed on the bright tiles – my mam was wrong; you don't automatically feel better after puking up. I rubbed wet out of my eyes, and just when I thought I'd forgotten about Mam's cancer it came thundering back to haunt me. The night was a black hole – I hoped she wasn't lonely. When I finally summoned the energy to get out of the cubicle, there was a bunch of girls complaining about the wait but I don't think it was aimed at me. I put on more blush as two girls squeezed in my cube, and I started not to look too bad in the pocked mirror. I was suffering though, half wanting to go back and shag Ben and half wishing I'd stayed home with Mam. I was blowing my nose in the sink when I realised I needed to pee. My head was whizzing round, and it felt like someone was battering me with a blunt object. I waited cross-armed for another stall to empty, all cold with nothing in me whatsoever. Eventually a door opened and I took the girl's place on the toilet – the seat had been completely hacked off; if I wasn't in a state I would've put down paper but who really cares. I dropped my undies then dropped my head. I cried til I wiped. I got out the poppers again to cheer me up, but all they did was crack my head open and make me feel paranoid. I realised I'd been more than half an hour in the loo, and when I walked through the busy club everything seemed misty and back-to-front.

Now Eve, this boy named Johnny said, and I hugged him slightly. You feeling alright?

I shrugged and I nodded – he got the idea. We whisked each other onto the dancefloor but without much conviction – Johnny was quite cute, but he knew my sister Laura and apparently he fucked loads of girls and forgot all about them. We didn't say anything for a while so I left him by the DJ box – I felt so crap about my mam, I thought I'd say something stupid to him and wake up with more stuff to worry about. I always wanted to know if he shagged Laura. Swanning round the dirty floor, I tried to find Ben or my friends but I just got stared out by random men and it annoyed the hell out of me. Some advice to boys: don't sleaze us. I felt arms go round me like spider legs and octopuses, and it was scary. I tried to shrug them off, tried not to break down on the dancefloor, kept my eyes peeled for Rachel's gold porn top and everything else. Tried not to cry when I spotted Jenni kissing Ben's head off. I turned away. Back upstairs I searched for Rach or Gracie or any old shoulder to cry on, but my eyes blurred too much. Wow, look how twinkly the lights look. I tried to do more poppers, but instead of making me electric I was a burst fuse – I was devastated. I could see slightly clearer in the dark, and I checked from the balcony it was really Ben and Jenni and it was. I raced back to the ladies' toilet, stopping on the way to look for the girls or the boy named Johnny at the DJ box.

Chapter Two

At the Traffic Lights

Adam

I had to shut things several times before I felt they were really closed. For example, that afternoon I had to shut the book we were reading, *Romeo and Juliet*, eight times before putting it in my bag, or else the school blows up. Miss Moore clocked me doing it, this mad grimace on her face as I heart-massaged the paperback, and I never went to another library lesson again. But worse than that, she once caught me slamming and reslamming the English door on the way to the toilet, and a little bit of piss did pop out. I saw this programme the other week about obsessive-compulsive disease, but I couldn't be bothered going to the doctors.

Since Friday I had all those fannies in my head, and I couldn't stop staring at Eve and Debbie. We had to draw self-portraits in Art after dinner – my page had on it hollow eyes, sunk cheeks and skeleton bones; what a sexy bastard. Mr Gray said it was abstract; I thought it was pretty heart-breaking. I had a sigh. I was always depressed. I pressed really hard into my eye sockets, accentuating the lifelessness and staring. Eve had drawn a cute blonde girl in crayon, slim with curvy lines in all the right places. The Prick scribbled a musclebound hunk with a massive bulge – did I mention he was also a total twat. Burny was a charcoal mess, but in real life everyone liked him – he had a bit of Italiano blood in him, and he was in the football team and all that shite. Donna was his trophy girlfriend but she wasn't drop-dead amazing – she always wore a red jumper with black tights, and she'd drawn a ladybird in colour pencil. I was positive they'd done all the rude stuff together – the Prick reckoned he shagged someone at Butlin's a year back, but it was probably his five fingers. He was a knob – as soon as he found out about sex off the Personal Development video he went round name-dropping 69s and creampies as if he did them every breaktime. But I was positive his only sex experience was pulling girls' pants down when we were young, and even now he was a pervy little cunt with a permanently smarmy fucked-up face.

Saying that, I was trying not to be seedy but something about Eve had my eyes magnified. She was by far the prettiest girl in any of my classes – gold highway hair, eyes like butterflies, and thighs to die for. I often fantasised drilling a wonderwall in the girls' shower but I didn't really have the tools for it. In her purple skirt Eve kept crossing her legs over and over, sometimes flashing a bit of skin underneath and I was getting ruffled. Her Lycra shorts reminded me of *Razzle*, but she was miles superior to those daft bitches. Whenever she looked over I pretended to be watching out the window, Marton Road all grey and green and I tried to see the trees slowly dropping all their leaves. When I pop my cherry the world will be a sunburst of petals. I hope it's me and her.

I imagined us quaffing wine in the finest restaurant; I'd have to swish it round my mouth and spit it in the bucket, and now and again Eve would touch me under the table while we twizzled our spaghetti. We'd suck it up together til we kissed in the middle, all the birds outside tweeting us a lovesong. I'd say all the right things and make her throw her head back with laughter. Then I'd take her to the cinema, holding hands and rubbing legs all through her favourite chick flick thing. We'd come out around ten o'clock, proceed to a club and dance rumbas til the lights come on – I'd buy all her drinks, and we'd kiss and I'd get that feeling in my stomach like a thousand lit candles. She'd introduce me to all her friends, and they'd fall in love with my sharp wit and charm and insist we marry and have lots of kids. I'd phone for a taxi at about 1:30, letting her have my coat as we walked in the cold to the rank. We wouldn't have to wait long, and I'd offer her a coffee at mine and she'd accept. We'd laugh at the innuendo and keep kissing until Easterside. After tipping the driver we'd watch the taxi soften in the distance, and I'd hug and whisper a sweet nothing in her ear. Bubbling inside I'd take Eve's hand, quietly unlock the front door, taking care not to rush or make her nervous. We'd kiss in the hallway, and kiss on the landing and all the way into the bedroom. She wouldn't laugh at all my crap lying around. I'd light incense, the dim light illuminating rose petals strewn across the four-poster bed. Instead of coffee I'd pop open a champagne bottle, sitting Eve down on the scented covers. Pouring a glass, we'd talk for hours about love and life until we both felt comfortable. I'd caress her smooth sumptuous skin like moonlight brought to flesh, and I'd put on two condoms if she wanted. Her bra would ping off without any trouble. And her knickers. I'd ask politely if she wanted me on top, taking care not to slather on her neck or bite her nipples or thrust too hard or not do any foreplay or anything else men always get slated for. I'd put on the Stones' 'She's a Rainbow' or 'Let's Spend the Night Together' and she wouldn't take it the wrong way, a rainbow being where the man gets period in his mouth and the girl gets cum in hers and they kiss. We'd writhe around to the humming guitars, our bodies like Plasticine slowly getting pushed together. As the room fills with flower smell, we'd slowly build momentum and climax completely simultaneously. Naturally, once she reaches orgasm twenty more times we'd stay up talking and cuddling til daybreak. And then the bell went.

Eve

My ex-boyfriend crashed at the traffic lights that dinner-time. He didn't explode like in the movies – Fairhurst accelerated into the back of the 63 Arriva, and the bus driver got slightly angry with him. Me and Jenni had nicked off school to get a sandwich from Greggs and a couple of Panda colas, and we were stood quietly in the frost when Fairhurst pulled up in his reddy Citroën. I still hadn't forgiven Jenni for stealing Ben at the Empire but I couldn't be cross for ever – I'd come to realise Jenni was a selfish cow ever since she stole the My Little Ponies from my fifth birthday bash. I yawned and blinked in the rain. It was your typical drizzly afternoon, and there was no point making it worse. Sniffing, I pulled my blue Duffer sleeves over the love-heart watch and bracelet, waiting patiently for the little green man.

Girls! Fairhurst shouted over the trancey sound-system; I didn't think he'd recognise me and Jenni in the middle of town with his windscreen-wipers working so fast. I wondered if I looked good with two black streaks across me.

How's it going, I said simply. I picked some cucumber out of my sandwich then popped it in my mouth, munching while I stared at his car, remembering those nights driving round Beechwood and Easterside with him on sex and wacky pills.

We found ecstasy in Year Nine. Me and the girls started getting it on a small scale from Fairhurst every other week, to take round someone's house and mess around or hang about the street. Everything changed – all at once we weren't fighting any more, we kissed each other, we said we loved each other and we had the best fun of our lives. The boys were that much sweeter, and depending on what night you did them school was a lot easier to bear. We knew something about being happy that our mams and dads and the other kids at school wouldn't understand.

It was about a year back when I lost my pill virginity, and I went and lost my other virginity and all. I remember Fairhurst picking me up early from Brackenhoe when I was meant to be in English with Miss Moore, the reddish Citroën bopping away on the side of Marton Road. Fairhurst used to love me in the sexy uniform, but I felt dead young to be going out with him, and I felt bad about missing lessons but I was no star at punctuation anyway. You alright? he asked me. I scampered down the school drive then jumped in the front, and Fairhurst was the kind of boy who gave you whiplash every time he put his foot down. I got pushed back in the racing seat as he spun the Citroën into the other lane. We headed for Belle Vue shops, and while Fairhurst talked to me about dance music and the

dole, occasionally he touched my thighs and I smiled.
Sometimes he went a bit further up than expected, but so
what. I wasn't sure whether to touch him back – we were
zooming round the roundabout at 40 mph, and there was
no point doing it just for the sake of it. The music was blistering and we could hardly hear each other. I had to fake
laughter at some things he said, and I was pretty blank-faced
when he brought up going to Whinney Banks for pills. I
guessed he meant drugs but I didn't want to embarrass
myself – all I'd done before was tac at this girl's house;
everyone said I was laughing and then I went white.
Fairhurst took us down Keith Road near where my house
was, but we carried on past the church and everything and
ended up in Acklam and hit a right. Sometimes he liked
showing off with wheelspins and stuff when we turned
corners, but it got boring after a bit and I had to pretend I
was impressed. Screech! I'd say in a dead girly voice, to
humour him. Fairhurst brought the Citroën into Whinney
Banks, through the bits with the run-down houses, and we
stopped on the corner of Sydney Close or somewhere. I
loved the name Sydney – if I ever got pregnant, I'd want to
call the kid that. Sitting in the front with the heater blowing, Fairhurst left me and went to one of the doors down
the close, walking like a daft arrogant monkey. He didn't
look hard at all. There was a big fuss with a lot of shouting
at each other from the upstairs flat, and I tried not to stare
when the front door unbolted and Fairhurst bolted in.
Those days in Middlesbrough they were doing a Dealer-A-
Day – you had to put a block of wood between the lock
and the stairway to stop policemen coming in. I tried to
occupy myself while Fairhurst got his prescription, flicking

through his cassettes and pretending I knew the names of DJs he scrawled on the boxes. Me and the girls had seen Judge Jules at Empire before, but who the hell was Laurent Garnier? He sounded like a perfume. A few young lads were prowling around while I stopped in the car – I hoped they didn't try to steal it with me inside. A few weeks before Fairhurst let me have a drive – we went to the incinerator, and I had a go with the biting-point and the blind-spot and the mirror-signal-manoeuvre thing and it was a good laugh. Supposedly the Citroën had been lowered and it had OZ alloys and a full-bore exhaust, but it wasn't any easier to drive. At least I didn't stall in front of my boyfriend, and if I had to I knew how to make a quick getaway from Whinney Banks. I'd be Ayrton Senna by the time I was seventeen, or someone else good at driving who wasn't dead. Whatever, Fairhurst came back in a minute, and we shot off again. He seemed a little uptight, but he stroked my leg once we were back in the Acklam Road traffic. I wanted to stop for a Twix at the shops, but I didn't want to take the piss. I shut my mouth and we drove all the way back to Easterside with the stereo blaring that little bit louder. Fairhurst slung a clear teeny bag on the dashboard, and I saw these tiny white pills with the picture of an apple on the sides. He asked if I'd ever done ecstasy before; all I could think of was all those girls it killed on the news. But it was exciting too, and we swallowed one down. Within ten minutes Fairhurst was parked up by Saltersgill field, and I was starting to feel a bit funny. I got him to switch off the blowers, and in a bit I had the dry mouth and the tingles we learnt about in Biology. It was exhilarating – Fairhurst stroked my skin and I shivered him up my spine. He turned down the music, and for

24

once I felt I could really talk to him – we joked about a load of crap, me getting all flustered and dreamy and open-mouthed. It was a beautiful school day – everything started to get more colourfuller, and everything felt like kitten's fur. Fairhurst looked so gorgeous I wanted to bite his face off, and I wasn't afraid to. Oh! His hands got quite flirty with me, but he checked I was feeling alright and I started rambling how amazing it was. I think he agreed; he was almost foaming at the mouth, and he popped another like they were Jelly Tots but I think he was showing off. He was beginning to go for my booby, and I knew he wanted to go further and I started saying how much I really cared for him and how we were meant for each other and all that shite. I had a few nerves even though the pill was unreal, but I just slid my legs open. He was grunting loads, and I watched as he unzipped and saw a knob for the first time. My mind was whizzing like a crazy person, but I took a hold of it anyway. When Fairhurst got those fingers in my knicks he didn't do the stabbing motions like Dan in the star tent; he was much softer, deeper and smooooth. What a star! I decided to take the bull by the horn – which other girls in Brackenhoe had ever lost their virginity on ecstasy? I tried to wank Fairhurst for a bit then we had oral sex, which is where the lady puts her mouth on the gentleman's rude bits. The end of his willy got a bit drippy, but none of that white gloop came out, thank god. I thought they were like water pistols? Looking back my technique in those days was crap – I thought you had to wank the shaft thing when in fact it was the end they all went mad for. Fairhurst slipped off my pants and said get on top of him. That meant I had to do all the work, and I shit myself for a second because I didn't want a baby with him. Maybe Fairhurst would've nailed me anyway if I hadn't mentioned it, but he seemed alright rolling on a Durex. It felt like shagging a plastic bag. At first I didn't want all of him in at once, but Fairhurst was obviously in ecstasy and I couldn't blame him for wanting to shag the arse off me. I remembered people like Claire taking the piss out of certain girls for just sitting like a corpse on their boyfriend's dicks, so I made a point of riding him like a cowgirl. My heart was banging. I started grinding my teeth as my skirt hitched up my belly, and my miaow was throbbing. It hurt in a nice way, but I had to stop him after a measly five minutes. Fairhurst seemed alright but I could tell he wanted more – there was no point ragging ourselves to bits though.

A year later, the car was still the same – shitty and noisy. Fairhurst drummed his fingers on the steering wheel, revving the engine miles too loud as we stood at the traffic lights, and he had to yell, So are youse two at school now?

Naw, these are our casuals, Jenni spurted, twirling in the uniform. I wasn't sure why she hammered Fairhurst so much, when it was him who used to take us into town when we were thirteen or fourteen. He bought us drinks and smokes for Jenni, and we never ever had a bad night.

Yeah, we are, yeah, I replied seriously, trying to be nice. Me and Fairhurst didn't really have bad blood, it's just I couldn't trust anyone in front of Rachel really. Not only did he have his hand on her tit at that party, he was tonguing her loads and that tongue was meant to be mine. Apparently Rachel reckoned she was off her trolley and couldn't remember a thing – she was a good girl, but just frustratingly magnetic to the opposite sex.

You want a lift? he asked. I nodded and jumped in the front with him, after a big mouth of cola then I chucked the can on the pavement. I finished off the sandwich as Jenni hopped in the back, feeling slightly like prostitutes with such an older guy but it was alright. I think Fairhurst recognised my tiny school skirt and started thinking to himself about the old days: he had his eyes on my thighs when he ploughed in the back of the 63. We all whiplashed forward and I banged my knee on the dashboard; Jenni smacked her hand off my headrest and she didn't even have her seatbelt on either. We were lucky. The wreckage wasn't that bad; Fairhurst's bumper caved in, and the bus got a tiny little scratch. I think the driver went easy on him because me and Jenni were there, but there was a bit of fuss about insurance and Fairhurst was pissed off about the bumper. I felt sorry for him as we finally rolled down Linthorpe Road, everybody staring and giggling and stuff. He meant something to me. I kept pretty quiet as Fairhurst edged the car around town, just thinking to myself about Saltersgill field. He patted my leg but that was it. I tended to throw away all the lads I ever liked, and it hurt a lot more than the knee.

Chapter Three

Once upon a Time

Virgin #1

You have to get fucked as quick as you can. From about age twelve you haven't got a choice about it. Me and Ste Barber and Matty went to this party with a tenner draw, thinking we could get some lasses paralysed and into bed with it. When we got there the house was packed with girls from Brackenhoe, and we helped ourselves to a bit of the wine and shit that knocked about. I kept grabbing at my sky blue Kappa trackies, feeling proper horny with the girls out of their school uniforms. Everyone looked mint without the crap baggy shirts and that. There were a load of them outside blowing up chuddy, and we set up a bucket watching them out the kitchen window. I cut the bottom off a Pepsi bottle that was lying in the rubbish, and we took the bucket out to do it with the girls. It was fuckin smart. I sat next to the Virgin, sprinkling on that bit extra so she got a good creamy one. Some of the girls hadn't done tac before – one of the blonde lasses got fuckin spaced out and turned green, but she didn't whitey or owt. The Virgin started laughing and messing about with us, and after I done another bucket she kept touching me and sprawling about. She was wrecked. We smoked a load more until about evening, and I was starting to see the colours and all that. By about sevenish we were laid out on the grass, feeling stoned as fuck. It was too much to move around – I got one of the girls to get us more cider, and I force-fed the Virgin it. They'd forgotten all about the chewy, and sooner or later everyone was off their face. My head was full of trippy shite, but then I remembered why we'd come to the party in the first place. I took another shot off someone's bucket, and the Virgin looked fuckin screwed to me. The plants in the garden were starting to flow about as she darted inside. I couldn't be bothered going after her, I figured she'd throw up then come back in a bit. But she never did. She passed out. Some of her mates put her to bed upstairs, laughing and joking about it but only because they were fucked. We all went to look at the Virgin dribbling sick on the pillow. Whoever's house it was, they said not to fuck about with her so everyone fucked off after a while. I was bursting for a piss, and when I got out the bathroom they were all gone. I crawled into bed with her – the bed was massive with teddies sat round the Virgin's head, and she looked fuckin nectar. The covers were going up and down with her breaths, and she was so drunk she thought I was her boyfriend. I said something reassuring to her, so she wouldn't panic and smash my face in. She had her eyes shut but I thought I saw her smile and I went to snog her – she tasted like sick and orange bubbly. She didn't hold back so I climbed on top of her and pulled back the sheets. The main thing was getting my end away rather than heating her up, so I didn't bother with any of that foreplay and I was fuckin hard as it was. The covers went up and down with my thrusts. She was sort of moaning as I fucked her undercover, and I groaned to spur her on a bit. I tried to see her tits, but it took ages

29

getting off her bra as we banged the bed against the wall. She was fuckin unresponsive, but then again it was her first time and she was passed out. Her cunt wasn't as tight as your own fist but you could sort of whack it along the top and get some sensation. She was so out of it I just messed about with her tits til I came. It was fuckin mint. Afterwards I left her as she was, getting in the mood for another bucket and I put back on the Kappas. We had a ton of that draw left, and I laid back in the grass doing nothing for the rest of the night. There were still a few girls sat around, getting drunk and getting sleepy, but I didn't have to get them wrecked any more.

Virgin #2

I wasn't a virgin. Sometimes I acted that way – like bringing the 4-pack of Hubba Bubba to the party instead of drinks – but I'd had sex tons of times. I gave a pack each to my Best Friends, and we stuffed our gobs with it. We blew up huge spheres in the dark, and we got drunk. We'd been in town for a couple of bevs before the party – we swallowed some vodka and cranberries at Chicago Rock then got the bus to Overfields or wherever the party was. It was a pretty big house and me and my Best Friend gave ourselves the grand tour, chasing each other round the bedrooms like knobheads = quite hilarious. Someone made a vat of wine and cider and spirity stuff in the kitchen, and everyone was helping themselves to glasses and getting really mortalled. Me and my Second Best Friend got dizzy really quick, and we sat in the garden drinking the punch and chatting up the boys. We blew up great big bubbles. My Third Best Friend always had a Pilot marker on her and she tagged her name round the garden, dark hair falling all about her face. The alcohol was obviously rushing round us, and it was about that time the Virgin came over. At first I thought his mates were going to soak us because they came out with a bucket full of water, but when you saw the sawn-off Pepsi bottle it was obvious they were doing drugs. One of them lit this bit of tac on the lid, then you saw the white smoke tornado up the bottle and they took a big hit on it. I laughed just watching. The boys made us have a go, and we were all up for it though we ended up getting ill. I had to take out the orange bubbly, and I felt my throat seizing up as I took the shot. The tac dried all the way up your oesophagus thing, and my head felt light and it kept getting lighter. The daisies were all spinning like ickle helicopters. I went to grab the Virgin's knee, and in the corner of my eye my Best Friend was laid out and laughing at the sky. I was getting pretty sick, and it was hard talking to the Virgin even though I liked him quite a bit. We'd known each other since primary school, and it was good having him around but my mouth was clammed and I was getting rather queasy. He made me drink more cider, which by now was tasting pretty sour but I necked it down. The Virgin had that dirty look in his eye, but I was tripping out and I could feel my cheeks leaking and I knew it was going to end in tragedy. I stood and shot to the bathroom, my Third Best Friend still tagging the windows and I couldn't even shout for help. I made it to the toilet and spewed all that punch out of me. It was like getting punched actually. I was still so dizzy and zapped of energy – someone or other helped me across the hall, or I fell asleep all by myself. I curled up in someone's made bed; the covers were patterned with daisies but I didn't give a shit. The bed felt so fat and comfy, though I could hardly sleep with my head whooshing and I dropped in and out of slumbers through the night. I dreamt up white boys and orange bubbles and white and orange flowers. Next thing I knew, there was a boy in the bed taking my flower. Or so he thought. My cunt was bone-dry, and he practically stabbed me to death. At first I imagined it was my boyfriend, and I swung my arms round his shoulders, completely dazed and off my rocker. I don't know when it dawned on me I'd been violated. Afterwards I dropped straight back to sleep, one tit squeezed out my new bra and my jeans halfway down my thighs = uncomfy. I guessed there'd be all that sludge in there. At about midnight I could hear my Second Best and Third Best Friend slagging me off, saying they'd have to take me to the clinic and calling me a slag and a slut. I felt so shit, and I didn't know what was up. I passed out again. I woke the next morning in a funny bed, the left booby still out and the undies scrunched and horrible. My Best Friends had kipped on the floor, and when I started stirring they shot up and rubbed their fuzzy heads. I felt sick and painful. I turned over in the bed, sorted out the bra and knicks, but my Third Best Friend started talking and it didn't sound like I was allowed to sleep. And it was a Sunday, of all things. We fixed up our clothes and hair, then tried to find the Overfields Girl whose house it was and let ourselves out. There were a few boys sleeping downstairs in a heap and we got out through the back, jumping over the punch bowls and the bucket. I felt depressed as anything on the Arriva, getting off at the clinic just to make it worse. We were hardly talking to each other as we walked, my Best

Friends all hungover and me probably all pregnant. I made a promise to shower the Virgin off me as soon as I got to Park End. Waiting in the clinic, it was my Second Best Friend who went up to the receptionist for the pill, and I bet she felt dead grown-up but she was a fucking virgin and all. I sat around but I wasn't thinking about my boyfriend – I wasn't thinking about anything really. Sighing, I swallowed down the pill then we made our way back home, through sunlight and trouble.

Chapter Four

Little Nicole

Eve

I jumped the baby up and down on my knee. I had on the pink pyjama bottoms and Baby Nicole was kicking the hell out of me in her tiny socks, getting over-excited. I stopped rocking her then pulled a face, blowing her a kiss – she looked so sweet in her flowery dress with her bulky nappy under; you couldn't imagine her getting shagged in a few years' time or doing white doves. All the boys'd fancy her – even I used to wear dinky sandals and frocks believe it or not. Smoothing out my jammy top, I yawned then leaned into the sofa, trying to watch *Friends* over Nicole's chubby cheeks. She was Mr and Mrs Davies' daughter from next door, and she was hilarious, gurgling and smiling whenever the audience laughed on TV. I always wanted a little sister. Laura probably had a different outlook, coming into the living room in her bathrobe and shivering.

You made tea yet? I asked, lying Nicole down on me. There were some pizzas in the freezer, but I couldn't be bothered pulling off the wrappers and finding out how to cook them. Laura looked at me with total disgust.

Naw, I've had mine, she snapped, so I ended up getting up and making a boring sandwich instead. Laura looked after Nicole while I slapped together bread and Philadelphia, chomping almost half of it before I was even back through the door. I knew I was pissing her off. I had the sandwich then grabbed the baby again, still feeling dead empty. The Davieses had taken out Mam and a few other dinnerladies from the Spacker School, to somewhere like the Viking or the Social. I didn't mind babysitting, but I had all this Maths coursework and I knew my teacher would rip my head off in the morning if I came without it. I shifted my weight, then smiled as Natasha breezed in. She was my other sister, and she was all done up in a turquoise dress with lots of back-combing and dirty blonde highlights. She waved fingers at Baby Nicole then made her dance on my lap, holding her podgy wrists. Natasha's pea-green nails looked seductive, and I made a mental note to steal some next time I went out.

Where you going? You look mint, I told her, as she peered her face out the window-pane. Peppermint, in fact.

Out with Dean, she replied. You stopping in all night?

Mmm. I nodded. Natasha was only nineteen, but she was already engaged to him – the ring was genuine gold. She wasn't pregnant or nothing; Dean was a good boyfriend and they'd been going out about three or four years without many break-ups. He didn't want to rush the wedding, but Natasha wanted Mam to be alive to see it and boys tended not to have a say on that kind of thing. I didn't know who was going to pay for it though, our dad not being on the scene too much those days – he had his own fancy-lady over in South Bank, but it wasn't like he absconded or anything. We still got on with him and saw him now and then, but all he ever banged on about round his was the new bird and the night shift at ICI and he was boring. Plus South

Bank could be scary, full of falling-down houses and angry young ruffians.

When you going out? I asked, and Natasha went, Dean's picking me up. We're going to Time I think.

Sniffing, I smoothed down the pyjama top then made sure Nicole wasn't choking herself to death on my thighs. She grumbled and flapped her arms when I lifted her to my chest, just as Dean's Escort dawdled past. Natasha peeked through the curtains again, then charged out of the house saying bye-bye then you heard the windy gales. I wished I was going out too. Natasha got a few whistles when she skipped across Beechwood Avenue, but they were most probably from Deano. It wasn't our fault for being so good-looking. We watched Natasha's back disappear, then the doorbell went and I wondered what she'd forgotten. I looked at Laura, but she was cosy and stubborn in her bathrobe so I got up and went myself. I handed her Baby Nicole then tugged the pink top over my belly, feeling a slight bit scruffy. It was only Rachel and Debbie and the boys though. Rach had swapped the gold porno top for white pyjamas with yellow elephants, and I smiled as they stood there clinking bottles. Gary and Dan looked quite alright under the dark grey sky, and I bit my lip when they stared me up and down.

Hiya, you coming out for a bit? Rachel asked. We've got drinks and that. Howay down the park.

Rachel nodded at the carrier then lifted out two big Bellabruscos. The other boys had a few bottles and all, and Debbie was clunking round a Tesco bag of spray-paint – it was a toss-up whether she was going to paint with it or huff it up. It did look like fun, but I rested a shoulder on the cream doorframe and said, I dunno. I'm meant to be babysitting.

Howay; it'll be a laugh, Dan said, and I wondered why he wanted me out so much. I bared my teeth then popped back through to the lounge, letting them in. Laura was sat tickling Nicole on the floor like a Munchkin, and she flapped her eyelashes at me then asked, Who's at the door?

It's Rachel and Debbie and that, I said, feigning an innocent face. I whispered sweetly, Is it okay if you babysit Nicole while I go out? I'll give you money and that.

God no way, Laura snarled. I was wanting an early night – she's yours.

Come on, I snapped back, and we were like two crocodiles in bedtime clothes. I grabbed Nicole from the ground, then went, I'll take her out with me then. It's your fault if she freezes.

Fuck off, Laura said, and she wasn't the swearing type. Mam'll kill you.

I already had on Nicole's peach Puffa coat and bobble hat, and we were out the door. I made sure I slammed it. I strapped Nicole in the fold-up buggy, then wheeled her onto the pavement while the boys stood there with high eyebrows. Me and Rachel charged off in our pyjamas.

Who's that? Gary asked, referring to the baby. He was always dead slow and docile on tac, and I wondered why anyone would really want to be like that – I was more the uppers girl. I looked at him and said, It's Jenni. She shrank.

I didn't really want Jenni in the conversation though. She only lived round the corner, and I didn't want her coming out in case I had a chance with Dan and I still wasn't very trusting of her. I linked arms with him while Rachel pushed the pram, and we walked softly between the stars and the estate. The sky was getting pitch-black like a planetarium. Me and Dan turned the corner at Deepdale Avenue then disconnected on the grass, Rachel trying her best to steer Nicole up the bump. That time of year the leaves were down, and we stood on the brown mush for a bit with nothing to do.

What you gonna paint? I asked Debbie, who was shaking up the Brilliant Red and Hot Pink. I wished I'd come out in my pink HOT CHICK socks. The best thing Debbie ever painted was the roundabout at North Ormesby, spraying each rung the colour of the rainbow so when it spun it roygbived round like a colour-wheel. She was artistic like that.

Just a throw-up or something, she replied, and I wondered if we'd throw up the Bellabrusco too. I laughed to myself. I didn't even know what a throw-up was. Rachel passed me the bottle while we watched Debbie outline wiggly pink then block it in, shaking that clickety sound in the cans. She was covering the back of someone's fence, and I wondered how she did it so speedy in the pitch-dark. I could hardly see Dan's pretty little face.

You two alright? I asked the boys, slinking around with their chins banging their tracksuit zips. They nodded. I swapped the Bella for Nicole again, then stood and pushed the pram back and forwards while cars shot past. Police often came round Beechwood looking for drug dealers and kids on motorbikes, but at least we weren't under the curfew. Those kids in Saltersgill must get bored silly. Anyhow, the streets were quite empty round here and all, and Debbie was always dead quick to nail her pictures. She was a blur like a señorita with maracas, and yet the word DEBE was always crystal-clear in the plasticky paint. Standing back, me and Debbie jumped around for a bit, half happy and freezing to death. I didn't know why we came out in our pyjamas so much – it was just a trend. I tucked my hands under the pink waistband, and I regretted it – I heard Gary thud fast on the soft grass, and he ripped down my PJ bottoms. Thank god for the Powerpuff Girl knickers. Everyone's mouths got massive and they laughed, while I pulled up the pants again and felt embarrassed. I called Gary a 4-letter word then chased him round the playing field til we got tired, and he let me grab his dick-pouch for revenge. He loved it – I didn't really dig my nails in though. We giggled loads at the other end of the field, then we hugged and he tried to grope my tits on the way back to DEBE's piece. We were all over.

God, I'm horny as fuck! Gary yelled, but it was no excuse. I laughed but I didn't let him touch me any more, instead standing next to the buggy and pretending to look after Baby Nicole. Rachel was all lovey-dovey too – her and Dan had snuggled up to the fence, away from the wet paint of course. They weren't kissing, but you could tell they were hitting it off with all that raucous laughter and body language. I thought for a sec if they'd dropped a pill together, since we knew loads of places round Grove Hill to get them and often it's an antidote to a boring evening. I made a mental note to check out their pupils. I poked out my dimples then tried to have a good time with Debbie, who was always up for fun and laughter when she was floating about. She was sky high on paint fumes – after a while we got her running around with a plastic bag over her head. I almost wetted the Powerpuffs. She looked like madness as TESCO sucked in and out with her breaths, and I'm surprised she didn't have a fit on the grass. When she pulled off the bag she had a huge beaming grin, and I squinted my eyes so much she was just teeth and colour.

So am I sleeping at yours tonight? Gary asked me, joking about. I raised a tweezered eyebrow and sniggered, Hmm. You come down from Park End tonight, like?

Yeah, Gaz replied. I tilted my head but I wouldn't shag Gary in a million years. He stinked and he shoplifted and he got into many a fight. Debbie liked him because they were in the same form, and often he stole paint for her from the car shops in town. He wasn't black enough for her, though. In fact he had an almost smack-white complexion. I shuddered watching him roll a special cigarette on his knees, the baccy stuff making me think of Mam. I kept my eyes on the cars zipping past, hoping she wouldn't catch me out with smokers and with Baby Nicole on top of that. I popped my head down and stuck my tongue out. All in all it was a weird night – me and Laura falling out, Rachel and Dan getting cuddly. Oh the sadness. I laughed and forgot all about it.

You want some of that? Dan shouted to me, holding out his Pulse cider. I took a swig then took a step back with his taste of fags in my mouth. I passed it back then pushed Nicole a little bit more – she was falling asleep even in the bitter cold and excitement. We hopped around the playing fields for a while longer, taking the piss and looking after each other as the sun fell off the earth completely. At about eleven I knew Mam would be home, and I imagined the Davieses worried sick and extremely cross with me. I was ready to head back, when the blue Fiesta pulled up and we saw the Jealous Girls.

Oi, dickheads! one of the girls shouted, sitting in the front with her spotty thick boyfriend. You look shit!

Me and Rachel glanced at each other, decked in pink and white with yellow elephants. The Jealous Girls were in our year at Brackenhoe, ugly pieces of shit from Saltersgill with dyed blonde hair and red cheeks like they'd been slapped. They were in the car with a couple of lads, and I gave the Fiesta the finger but they wouldn't shift.

Fuck off you, Rachel yelled back, and she made me smirk.

You what? another Jealous Girl shouted from the back. They thought they were so smart driving round Keith Road and Belle Vue with dopey Aids carriers, and I grinned because our lads were so much nicer than theirs. Even Gaz looked dreamy in comparison. He was always up for aggro, and he strode up to the car spouting, You heard, you daft cunt.

Check all youse out, coming up here thinking you're dead hard, the Jealous Girl in the front said, as we followed our Gary on the muddy grass. I did admire his confidence, and I laughed when he went, Yeah well check youse out in that fuckin piece of shit.

At least we've got a car, the Jealous Girl said – you could tell she was shagging the lad in the front; his hand was practically down her Donnay trousers, and hers was on his gearstick. Urgh, Donnay trousers of all things.

Youse can shut up. That was his contribution. I pulled the pink top closer to my chest – you could see the boys in the Fiesta fancied us more than the Jealous Girls, but they could dream on. I was sometimes up for a bitch-fight, but all I did while everyone talked was push Baby Nicole around in the grass. I didn't want her getting involved.

Fuckin starting? Gaz went, confronting that ugly cunt. I

hoped she couldn't hear the dirty words. Gary nearly stuck his face through the window, and you could sort of see it coming when the Jealous Girl lunged and dug her nails across it. He reeled backward, and we all flinched for him. The driver said then, Howay we'll run them over!

He revved the engine dead loud and I glanced at Debbie, who was stood worryingly behind them. But it was funny – I loved stupid threats like that. I imagined the car full of Jealous Girls off-roading pathetically on the playing field, trying to round us all up and splat us across the grass. I hid my smile in the neck of the pyjama top. It was chilly. Me and Rachel linked arms with Dan as the Fiesta reversed, then brum-brummed as if it was going to come at us but we just stood and watched. Gary was all rashed on his cheek where the Jealous Girl had lashed out, and you imagined all the sperms and muck and poo she had under her nails. The Girls were always trying to out-do us, but with the boys around you couldn't be afraid of a shitty G-reg. In the end the Fiesta just wheelspinned off down Deepdale – it was pretty obvious they wouldn't bring it on the field; it would've fallen apart. As the car drove off there was a sad kind of feeling – it was very very late. I sighed and sighed. In the splashes of streetlight, you could just about see DAFT BITCHES sprayed on the boot of the Fiesta in hot pink and Debbie grinned as she clicked the cap back on. It stood out, pink on sky blue. We stared and we rolled around on the grass.

Adam

I lived in the ceiling with naked girls. I was first home on Thursday, and I grabbed a torch and Dad's *Razzle* and climbed into the attic with my school uniform still on. I took up a tub of handcare cream. It was pretty dusty, and I sat amongst the Christmas decorations and a load of insects round my head. I didn't know what was dirtier, being in the loft or having a big wank with my trousers and boxers down at four o'clock in the afternoon.

I had an okay day at school. The only thing I looked forward to at Brackenhoe was either hometime or seeing luxurious girls. Sometimes I wished they were from Beverley Hills or Dawson's Creek instead of Berwick Hills or Doggy, but one smile or one word from someone like Rachel, Eve, Abi etc. could change your day. They blanked me at dinnertime, but on the way to fifth lesson I smiled at Debbie Forrester and for the whole of Double Science I was riding on a unicorn. Girls and music were the only things keeping my head screwed on. I smiled as I flicked the *Razzle* pages, all those girls sitting around with their bums in your face. You tried not to check for muck or hairs or anything, instead imagining yourself getting on with them and getting off with them. Now and then you had to put yourself in the same position with real girls from Brackenhoe, although I knew they'd already been shagged by people like Gary Clinton, Dan or Ste Barber – the arrogant, naughty cunts. I hated them. That morning Gaz barged into me just because I had to shut the Art Materials drawer four or five times.

There was a thud and a click in the hallway, and my parents came through the front door talking like birds. My heart popped out, and I almost stopped wanking but I'd just reached Danni 19 London and she had a great story about shagging her sister's boyfriend on the Costa del Sol. I got the cream out from between my fingers. I made sure I didn't creak the timbers, and I didn't say a word when my mum shouted upstairs, 'We're back!'

I gulped then turned back to Danni 19. Mum and Dad might think I was out having fun, but really I was wanking in the attic. I tried not to moan as I got to that point with the white fountain. I could hear mumbles and grumbles through the floorboards, and I started to wonder how I'd get away with it but me and Danni 19 could keep a secret. She was great-looking for someone in such a filthy mag, and I wondered how it felt for her in front of all the cameras with her parts out. She seemed to be smiling, but all the time you must get sleazed by the crew and taken advantage of, and I hated that about boys. Her blue eyes and my hazels connected through the dark, and all the insects slowly started dancing round us as I reached the boil. I probably would've spunked if it wasn't for my dad coming through the roof. The light bounced in like a gigantic awful glowworm and I shit myself. His hands appeared first then his head and the rest of him, and he had a double-take before clocking me and the porno mag. I yanked up the school trousers and I tried to shut it seven times but Danni 19 just stared out of the book and pouted. She was supposed to be my mate. I wondered if Dad had heard me creaking from downstairs or if he realised his porno was missing – he pretended not to recognise it as he grabbed me. The bugs scattered. Dad growled something not very nice, then went crazy and threw me across the loft. If it makes a difference, I didn't feel so turned on any more. I wanted to die. He yelled something or other, then nearly ripped my ear off as he yanked me through a cloud of dust. All I tried to do was guard my head, pushing at him with one freezing cold hand and one hot clammy hand. I felt my foot smash through my bedroom ceiling, between the timbers where it was dead weak, and Dad got angry at that and punched me rock-hard in the face. I landed on the woodbeams. He came at me again with his steel-caps, me curling up and crying quite a bit but I wasn't bleeding. He grabbed the *Razzle* then kicked me out the attic hole. I was screaming loads but luckily the step-ladder eased my fall as I went flying, and I thudded on the beigey carpet. I made a big performance, rolling around pretending to be dead, but Dad just rumbled down the steps and off to his bedroom. I didn't get up til ages afterwards – I wanted to get back at him but it was more my style to lie around and feel sorry for myself. He kicked past me a few times and I didn't get my tea. I wept a bit and wrapped myself round the step-ladder, and after an hour and a half I figured it was the ladder standing there that gave it all away.

Chapter Five

Sun

Adam

The bad times snowballed then. I was starting to get those demonic thoughts in my head like Charlie Manson listening to the White Album for the first time, and that night I stuck 'Revolution 9' on the repeat setting. Rise! I'd been to sleep with my clothes and headphones on, and rolled out at about seven o'clock with the red room ice-cold and creepy around me. The bump on my temple was green. The hole in the ceiling was gigantic. I didn't want to hang around for my parents, so I pulled on a cream beanie and slid down the stairs. The hat hid the bruises alright, though I'd probably get killed for it at school.

I considered getting some breakfast but I couldn't face bumping into them. Instead I jumped into black Clarks, pulled on the Nike bag, and decided to walk around the estate for a while on my own. I took Disc One out with me, and as it kicked in I started to feel right. There was no one about. I had almost an hour before I had to call for the Prick, and there was a nice morning out there waiting for me. It was shiny bitter silver, and I paced down Broadwell Road with the sunlight pinging in and out from the semi-detached houses, the only other people around dressed in odd track-suits walking skinny ratty dogs. It was both sad and happy. I felt dead vulnerable, like a cat with a few of its lives gone or a Russian doll with a couple taken out. And I thought one word from anyone would crack me, but the animals and crispy wind were by my side. I listened to 'Dear Prudence', John telling me not to be a recluse when there's sun and fun-shine outside and things to do. I walked onto Saltersgill field, and despite the dogshit, needles and dodgy characters there were at least daisies and dandelions and running water. And I walked and walked down past the banks of the stagnant beck, staring at the playing fields going gold and green and that's when I realised all the suffering was over.

But the suffering wasn't over at all. On the way to school the Prick teased me about the beanie and the swelling, and I forgot I'd have to explain it to everyone. I told him I got thumped outside Easterside shops, and it was a regular occurrence but I felt crap. The sun was beaming out but I felt compressed. I switched off the Discman and I tried not to cry while I walked with him. The Prick was one of those friends you'd blow off if only you hadn't grown up together. Everything to him was a piss-take, and as we went thundering down Marton Road he kept thumping and roughing me up, as if to prove he would've been alright in the same situation. It suddenly felt a lot colder, and when we got to Brackenhoe everyone was just as irritating in the form room. Abi complimented the Top Man beanie, but a load of kids I didn't really like were going on about the green bumps on the side of my bonce. I slumped on the plastic seat and didn't speak anything to anyone.

We had History at half-nine on the top floor, and I watched the skyline strobe-light now and then – it was so sunny, the grass was bright blue and the grey buildings dripped pink. I tried to surround myself in friends and get through the next twenty-four hours, but I didn't have all that many friends. I was wallowing in sadness under a big blue duvet cover. I sat with the Prick and he borrowed my pen to drum something on the tabletop, showing off. I kept my eyes outside. The Prick thought girls would go for him if he came across as some amazing rock star, but he was complete shite. Eve and Rachel Shannon were sat chattering in the back, and they weren't noticing either of us. The Prick started to blast out this simple 4/4 beat, and when I heard one of the pens smash to bits it was obvious God would choose my fancy Papermate over the Prick's blue Bic. There were a few giggles, but instead of getting wet eyes again I just crossed my arms and blocked it out. The Prick was laughing in my face; the worst part was thinking of Mum buying the stationery for me all special, but they were only pens. I blew out. He was still a fucking prick though.

'Quiet!' Mr Barley yelled loudish, coming in with another guy he introduced as Sergeant McAllister, dressed all in army attire and the regulation haircut. The Prick said a joke about fancy dress but it didn't tickle me. Straight away the Sergeant spotted the girls at the back, he smiled and winked in a dead frustrating way. He seemed like a total cunt, but I was scared of his musclebound physique.

'Alright now,' he said, with a mixture of flexed biceps and bright beacon eyes. 'I'm here to talk to youse about the army. I understand youse are coming to the end of the year now, and you're wondering what direction youse might be wanting to take . . .'

Sergeant McAllister went on like that for about forty minutes, and it was hard not to daydream. A life away from home building up strength and firing guns sounded superb, but only since my dad caught me having a wank. There'd been other violent occurrences where my dad was concerned – this one time I broke a china plate and he put my head in the microwave (which didn't work), then another time I ran off the hot water having a shower and found myself hanging out the bathroom window by my tootsies (which did work). I shit myself. But on telly the army looked a bit too close to prison, scrubbing shoes and eating bollocks and getting shouted at, and I doubted I'd even pass the medical. I switched off and stared really blank into outer space. As you'd expect, the Prick pretended to be totally engrossed, but he wanted to be a holiday rep when he grew up. He scribbled down loads of notes in the back of his History book, trying to look macho but I saw through it. He was a blonde fucking dwarf. I pulled my shirt sleeves over my hands, then put down my head and had a few thoughts on the polyester. I imagined Dad flying against the wall as I unloaded a couple of rounds on him, lots of blood and guts and bang bangs.

'I hope you're taking notes, lad,' Sergeant McAllister blurted out, and I flinched. I wasn't sure if he was talking to me, but when I looked up bubbly-eyed everyone was sniggering. I shook and grabbed for my notebook, spiting the Prick because his wild scrawling made me look even worse. I flicked to the back, then stared and went shyly, 'I need a pen.'

'Drop and give me twenty!' the Sarge yelled, but you could sort of tell he was joking. What a cock. I probably would've done it if it wasn't for Eve in the back though.

'Twenty what?' she mumbled, and a few of her mates giggled. I smiled, and I still felt bleary when she offered, 'Here, Adam, I've got one you can lend.'

She tossed over a silver twisty ballpoint, and I grinned icebergs as I grabbed for it, and scribbled a cartoony GI Joe with a dick on his head and a fat gut. He wouldn't give up, though. He threw a filthy flirtatious face at Eve, and said, 'Oh you're such a sweetheart, aren't you. Haw haw. Look at him; he'd never make it in the army anyway. He's been fighting with his sister again.'

Next time he talks to me in the third person his face is going through the blackboard. I brushed him off with a little nod, but the kids were killing themselves and I could feel myself getting mental. I had to keep repeating 'Dear Prudence' in my head, clamping together my thumb and middle finger in the meditation stylee. I didn't have a happy place though. My head felt messy, but Eve was clearing it up like a maid with a feather-duster, though I stopped myself from making that image too French and exotic.

'Actually it was my dad; he beats me up all the time,' I said in my head. I shifted in my seat, then wrote a couple of words now and then while the bastard carried on, dropping off to sleep but with eyes open. I made a vow to grow muscles, and get out of the house more. I half-smiled and held on to Eve's pen for the rest of the morning, feeling alright. Outside, white rainbows erupted and poured out twinkling waterfalls. It was a beautiful day, and it was the only thing keeping me from topping myself. We spent dinnertime in the sun, me and the Prick chewing Astrobelts while we walked around, Burny and Donna cuddling in the canteen with the rays burning through the glass. We stepped on shadows. After a while Abi caught us up from the playground, and she gossiped and I kept fondling Eve's pen like a little doll's leg. Even though she was our best friend, I couldn't help checking Abi out as we strolled about, boys always thinking about sick stuff and girls' lumps and bumps. I remembered going out with her in Easterside Primary and having our first kiss in a tree in Stewarts Park. She was fun to be with, swishing the dark hair while she nattered about lasses from Beechwood and criminals and that. Me and the Prick laughed at everything. I was getting in a good mood, and I floated around looking for Eve. Like an angel exploding in a starburst, she was the only thing on my mind from then onwards. We saw Rachel Shannon hanging with a load of boys at the main entrance, getting hounded, and I guessed she couldn't be far away.

'She's fucking mint,' the Prick said as we dodged mud and litter, but Rachel didn't catch it. 'I'd do her all over.'

'That's my fucking cousin!' Abi whispered, then winked as we went past the group. Funny how those two were related, Rachel being a Swedish pornstar and Abi almost spic in appearance. As we went a little further round the main building, down by the pyramids, I suddenly spotted supergirl Eve and her mate Debbie laid on the grass and I felt again for the silver pen. They were sunbathing with their shirts half undone, and in the flashing light I thought Eve was waving me over with her tie but I was in a bit of a daze mind you. I decided to head over anyway and give back the pen. I always figured her and Debbie were the sweeter ones of the group, but they still could've told me to fuck right off. I made arrangements to meet the Prick and Abi in the form room later on – they were already halfway down the concrete, flirting in the light bits and dark bits. I watched the sun-kissed goddesses roll over a couple of times. And I walked and walked down past the concrete and clover patch, staring at the playing fields going gold and green and that's when I realised all the suffering was over.

Butterfly

The sun came out on Friday and so did I. I stirred in the cocoon, and out of the blue a crack was forming. The light began to burst in, and with a bit of wriggling I squeezed out of the sleeping-bag and blinked my eyes at the world. My blue wings were soaked, and I shivered a little bit then rubbed my antennae and had a yawn. God I needed that. I read in the handbook you have to dry your wings thoroughly before flying off, so I sat about looking at things and being bored. Until I spotted the two girls sunbathing. They were more goose-pimpled than tanned, though – it was pretty freezing. It started to dawn on me I must've woken up too early, but I took advantage of the rays and fluttered them wings. I wouldn't mind getting back to bed, but when I turned round on the clover the chrysalis had shrivelled up and blown off. I sighed then squinted as the boy wandered across the grass. I wished he'd keep his head up and not be so self-conscious about the bruises, though. On such a shiny day, there was nothing to be down about.

'Hiya,' Adam said shyly once he reached us. 'I've got your pen.'

'Oh, right,' was all Eve could say, frowning. I nearly laughed because she didn't seem interested in him, and there was a funny silence. I was getting dizzy stood head-down, but in an hour or so I'd be young, free and single. It was exciting. Adam pulled a silvery pen out of his pocket and handed it to her – I caught a glimpse of myself in the reflection. I was incredible blue with glitter-glue wings – I knew it was worth getting teased when I was a sad green caterpillar. I was so ecstatic I could've jumped off the clover right there and then, but in the end I didn't want to show off or die.

'Thanks,' Eve said, buttoning up her school shirt.

'So, how are you doing?' the boy asked next, and you really had to feel for him.

'We're fine, aren't we,' Debbie giggled, crossing her legs on the rough grass. 'You revised for that test yet?'

'The Science?'

'Yeah.'

'Nah, not really,' Adam replied, but you could tell he had. 'It alright if I sit for a bit?'

The girls laughed and nodded. They shuffled to one side and cleared a space for him on the running-track, then Adam pulled off his coat and sat down on it cross-legged. He kept his head down and pretended to tighten his laces, then eventually asked, 'So what youse been doing down here? Just sunbathing and that?'

'Yeah,' Eve said, clenching a fist round her high ponytail. 'As you can see, we're golden-brown.'

It was an excuse for me to look down their shirts, but Adam was too polite for all that. Debbie laid her chin on her knuckles – next time I was going to be reincarnated a teenage girl. She rolled over and she sighed, 'I'm hungover.'

'You go out last night?' Adam asked, raising his eyebrows.

'Nah, just went round my boyfriend's. Dead knackered.'

'You ever go to pubs and stuff?' he asked next as Debbie took Eve's pen and wrote her name really fancy on her hand. Being a butterfly I wasn't much into graffiti. I sighed and glanced into the distance as Eve replied, 'Yeah, we're always going down Easterside and that. Last Friday we went to Empire, which was decent.'

'Eve spewed,' Debbie butted in, and everyone laughed their heads off; even me. I crawled across a four-leaf clover, watching out for birds overhead. It'd be just my luck to survive winter, but get munched by a birdy. Bright blue wings weren't exactly my idea of camouflage neither.

'Poor thing,' Adam said softly, sliding closer to the girls on his bum. He should've touched her then, but instead he looked at the floor again and stayed quiet. Eve shone a look at Debbie, and they smiled. They leaned back to get more sun, and Eve even undid some of her buttons again. It was getting heated. Adam wasn't sure where to look, but he flared teeth and added, 'I'd go out too, but my mates aren't really into it.'

'We see Jason Burn and Donna out quite a bit, like. You should get yourself out with them,' Debbie said, twizzling the Biro on and off in her pink-coated nails. 'What were you up to last night? Looks like you've been in the wars.'

Adam suddenly went inside himself and sat up all jerky, his hands in the grass. All you could see was his cream beanie, and he mumbled, 'Just got into bother at the shops.'

'Who was it?' Eve asked, swishing blonde hair about. 'I've got a cousin who'd knock them out for you. It's no hassle. There's so many dicks about.'

'Nah, you're alright,' Adam replied, getting redder. He sniffed and ruffled his hair underneath, then quickly changed the subject. 'So, youse going out tonight?'

'Dunno,' Eve said, keeping the sun out of her eyes with her hand, like a gorgeous captain out at sea. 'See how I feel.'

'If you ever see us out and about,' Debbie started, 'you'll have to buy us a drink or something.'

Adam sniggered, then started to look uncomfortable again and stood up. He was no Cary Grant. He slowly picked up the Adidas jacket; other school kids were walking up the field and the bell was about to go. He was probably desperate to get swotting away again. Blinking, he shoved the coat on and for a second he looked like a red admiral. I was slightly horny – flexing my claspers, I racked my brains and hoped it wasn't butterflies who ate their husbands.

'So aren't you seeing anyone, Adam?' the girl asked, folding up her Duffer top and cardigan on the grass, which were strewn about.

'Naw, not yet,' Adam said, and he got flustered again. What an unusual person. 'Are you?'

'No; young, free and single,' Eve laughed; that was my line. I wavered on the clovers. Eve dipped her head back and stared at the fluffy clouds. The sky was so massive I trembled at the thought of flying into it, but it did look tremendous.

'I'm sure you'll get someone nice,' Adam said, zipping up. He was so selfless – you could tell that. 'Anyway, I guess I'll love you and leave you now. See youse later.'

'Bye-bye,' the girls said together, waving him off. Eve watched him stride past the steel fence, then played with the studs in her ears and said, 'Aww, he's nice, isn't he.'

'Yeah, he's funny,' Debbie said. I flapped the neon wings again, but they weren't getting any drier. I breathed out then jiggled about. I only had twenty-four hours to find a mate – it was nerve-wracking, maybe the girls hadn't even hatched, but who really could turn down sparkly sequin wings and big old claspers.

'Look, there's a butterfly,' Debbie said, pointing me out just as they got up to leave. I felt my cheeks glow. I was

flattered but I didn't flutter much longer. As the girls continued chatting and stomping up the playing field, a huge
blackbird suddenly swooped out of nowhere and gobbled
me up. I screamed and screamed – his beak was like a chain-
saw, and I couldn't escape it. I curled up then dropped to
the ground, two glitter-blue arms on the grass and two little antennae on the wind.

Eve

Glitter-blue splashed the water. It burnt! You always seem to
get so relaxed and vacant before bathtime, only to get scald-
ed. I hid about in the Boots bubbles, getting numb after a
while and quite steamy. Me and Laura had the bridesmaid
dresses hung above the door – these off-white numbers
with no straps and fairly short. She was in there with me
chattering about all sorts. We had butterflies flying round
our tums. Eventually I just gave in and ran some cold, then
I swished around and used the old sponge, the one like a
shard of glass or breezeblock but it definitely got you
sparkling. I squeezed my hair back against my head – it
always looked darker wet, but by ceremony time me and
Laura would be blessed with platinum blonde ringlets. I was
speaking foam. As the steam rose and swirled, Natasha
knocked and appeared in her gorgeous wedding dress, and
we had to stop what we were doing and stare at her.

You look amazing, I said. It'd been a hectic day – all the
wedding arrangements had been sorted before Christmas,
but there was still the important matter of looking great.
Laura started to put on the dress while Natasha checked her
make-up – the fake tan looked really over the top in her
white gown. I smiled and watched Natasha pout four or

five times, ready for the you may now kiss the bride part.

Who are you bringing again, Laura? she asked, turning round. I dipped my head underwater when she replied, Some lad.

Anyone nice? I asked, but I wasn't bothered. She told me a little about this boy from Kirby College with blue eyes and big muscles, but I just stopped and glared at the water. I dripped Fructis shampoo on myself, hoping they wouldn't come home together and moan moan moan through the night. At least we were getting rid of Natasha and Dean. Five nights a week they banged the bed up against my head, but I didn't really mean that. I thought back to me, Natasha and Laura sharing the bathtub on Sundays, Mam and our Dad running upstairs every five minutes to check we hadn't drowned. We used to have competitions for holding our breath underwater and flooding the bathroom sliding up and down it, but we wouldn't go that far. I massaged round the shampoo then ducked in again, squinting as the shampoo dissolved all over. My hair rose to the surface, and I stopped like that til Laura belted out, Eve, have you still got that necklace I like?

Trying to speak underwater, a load of bubbles made a noise, then I leapt to the surface and said, What?

Have you still got that nice necklace? she repeated, as I stretched out of the water and covered myself with one arm.

The chunky gold thing? I asked, lowering in again.

Yeah; can I borrow it?

Er, yeah. It's in my blue box.

Is it really gold? Natasha asked as she left the room, raising one eyebrow she'd retweezered.

Well no, it's all rusty now. But you know what I mean.

57

Shutting my eyes, I leant back in the tub and rinsed off the shampoo completely. The lavender foam faded into cloud. Then I shimmied forward, pulling my knees up to my chest and watching out my hair didn't land in the dirty water. For a bit I stared as Laura came back and did her make-up, throwing round reds and pinks and blacks and peaches. I smiled, getting to that horrible point of forcing yourself out of the bath. I sat there like a jelly blancmange, and fortunately just then Mam came through the door with cups of tea so I stayed put. God, it was getting crowded – in these terrace houses the bathrooms are practically a broom cupboard. Mam had on a new two-piece from Binns with these tiny flower motifs and she was looking well. She smiled and passed over my Tigger mug.

Thanks, I said.

Roundabout then Mam was well into the chemotherapy, but luckily you could wear a hat to the wedding. She was still herself really. Supposedly the therapy was quite harsh – I didn't know too much about it, did they zap you with a laser gun? We didn't tend to go into it much; instead we always tried to stay happy. I gurgled the gorgeous tea then flashed eyelashes at my mam. It was getting late but I couldn't get out of the bath at all, and I made sure that tea lasted. I was absolutely boiling, but for the sake of it I decided to have another scrub in the murky water. Looking at myself in the nud always made me think of Fairhurst – he preferred girls to have a totally bare miaow, and now and then we shaved each other round his. I shaved him just for the laugh of it. I always made sure to keep my parts dead fresh – you get more cuntilingus from boys that way. How good is sex! I was starting to feel pretty silly and immature, so I sat up straight and polished off the tea. Mam took my mug back downstairs, and under the cowgirl hat you couldn't tell she didn't have any hair.

Don't be too long in that bath! the kitchen echoed. You don't want to be wrinkly for the wedding, do you.

Sighing, I grabbed one side of the tub then asked Natasha, Can you pass me the big one, please?

I pointed to the massive goldfishes towel slung over the radiator, then I pulled the bath-plug and felt the water drain around me, leaving a bit of candy-floss on my skin. Natasha threw the rug at me as I stood up, and I glimmered in the white light. It started to feel cold out of the bath-water so I fixed the towel round and laughed when the plug-hole burped behind me. Using a different towel for my hair, I sat on the edge of the bath then waited for Laura and Natasha to finish at the mirror. I was well behind schedule for the pampering, but it was good jumping into the dress straight after a scrub. The silk was like a second layer of skin, and I decided to go commando. Outside the town was clouded over, and the whiteness of the window shone through at us. I stood for a bit tucking into Laura's toiletries, and I couldn't imagine how it must feel for Natasha – she was about to spend the rest of her life with one boy. God knows who I'd end up with. My outlook was not to worry about it too much, just enjoy your life because you've only got one of them. Some girls at Brackenhoe were already settled down with a fella, some had a kid or two, and some were just plain boring. But Natasha and Dean were amazing together, and the main thing was Mam seeing at least one of us tie the knot. On the way downstairs we felt like princesses and we floated outside – the taxi came at eleven. I hoped Natasha got the sun.

Chapter Six

Levonelle

Claire

I don't know when it dawned on me I'd been violated. Afterwards I dropped straight back to sleep, one tit squeezed out my new bra and my jeans halfway down my thighs = uncomfy. I guessed there'd be all that sludge in there. At about midnight I could hear Rachel and Jenni slagging me off, saying they'd have to take me to the clinic and calling me a slag and a slut. I felt so shit, and I didn't know what was up. I passed out again. I woke the next morning in a funny bed, the left booby still out and the undies scrunched and horrible. Rachel and Jenni had kipped on the floor, and when I started stirring they shot up and rubbed their fuzzy heads. I felt sick and painful. I turned over in the bed, sorted out the bra and knicks, but Jenni started talking and it didn't sound like I was allowed to sleep. And it was a Sunday, of all things. We fixed up our clothes and hair, then tried to find the Overfields Girl whose house it was and let ourselves out. There were a few boys sleeping downstairs in a heap and we got out through the back, jumping over the punch bowls and the bucket. I felt depressed as anything on the Arriva, getting off at the clinic just to make it worse. We were hardly talking to each other as we walked, but Jenni kept reminding me about

Clinton. It hurt to remember them calling me names the night before – I'd been with about five or six boys before, but never been unprotected before now and I sometimes went to the docs for checks and things. Jenni was making out I'd never seen a clinic before in my life, but fuck her. In fact I doubted she'd ever seen any action in her life. It wasn't my fault – it was just the same as her going out and getting off with lads for drinks, or that time she sucked someone's knob outside the Bongo. I hardly ever went out because of the epilepsy thing – I had a few seizures when I was younger, and in any case I didn't have the money to go out gallivanting all the time. It's not like one flashing light sets me off, it's just I wasn't into all the drugs the girls were doing, and ecstasy tended to go hand in hand with strobe lights. As we sloped towards Henry Taylor Court and the scruffy bungalows, my head was banging off of that bucket and all the drinking. At one point Rachel's phone beeped and she stared at it and clicked for ages. We soon got to the clinic and it looked so uninviting – we strode through the doors quite slowly with faded faces. I yawned – Jenni wanted to do all the talking, so me and Rach stood around with just the posters of dicks and fannies to look at. My tummy flipped over, and I felt so faint I had to plonk myself next to some skinny lad in a red and white Von Dutch cap. He was slightly hot, but I didn't speak a word because he was probably crawling with Aids and I didn't want to push it. I knew Jenni and Rachel were doing me a favour but it was long and drawn-out like water torture – if I'd been in the same situation on my own, I probably would've just crept home and figured I'd be alright. Nothing like pregnancy or STD or cancer is ever going to touch you. Biting my red nail, I slouched on the seat and gazed at the carpet. In a minute Jenni called me over, and the nurse-person said I had to take one pill now and another in six hours or whenever it was. It seemed a bit overboard but I swallowed down the first one and I felt a bit better already. After all, they were only trying to catch one tiny sperm creature. 'Thanks,' I said, half to the nurse and half to Jenni and Rachel. I was all clear, but I baulked slightly seeing a horrible foetus thing on the wall. I made plans to do some laundry and get showered back in Park End, and we strode out of there with slightly sunnier faces. Rachel swung off her cheerleader jacket, Jenni lit a superking, and I flicked hair out of my sleepy peeps. Jen and Rach had to wait for another Arriva, so I waved bye-bye quite cheery and sat alone on the first Stagecoach down Ladgate Lane and swept across Park End. The pink tower-block was lush in the sunshine, and I watched for people's faces in the many windows but you never quite caught them. It must've been after noon when I got off, and I said thanks to the sulky driver then walked my way to Delamere. I thought our health centre on Overdale Road looked awful pretty all of a sudden. Our Shaun was charging round the front yard in a Robin outfit when I reached the house, and he hardly even saw me because he was screaming so much. Step-dad Dave was watching out the top bedroom window, and I rubbed Shauny's glossy hair then slipped inside. Our lawn was pretty battered, and I tramped in a little mud before kicking my Ellesses on the pile. The boy-wonder carried on playing and I left the door ajar for him, smiling when he shrieked hi to me. 'Hey you,' I replied, then stormed upstairs quite sharpish for that shower. I shouted hello at Joe's bedroom door then Dave and Mam's, getting a couple of replies before peeling off my top and other bits in the bathroom. I hated Dave leaving all his underduds around, and I kicked them outside as the room steamed up. I ripped off earrings and scrubbed off make-up, chucking everything on the side then diving into the red-hot waterfall. I frazzled those sperms = Batman and Robin would've been dead proud. Pow! And zap! I ran the water into my mouth. As it hit me I started to feel a little odd, not epileptic but very, very weary and dodgy. I stood about and breathed, and suddenly I realised how fucking hungover I was. All the commotion at the clinic had sort of blocked it out, and I tried to sit down on the edge and I was tempted to just spew up all over the bathroom. That always worked a treat. For a bit I sat there shaking, the water clashing off the white panels, and I thought fuck it – I retched and puked chocolate milkshake down the bath. At least it wasn't in my room. I hoiked my legs up on the tub sides til the spew drained away, feeling better although it'd been a shitty day and tears were starting to clot my eyelashes. And then I heard the morning-after pill clatter down the pipes. Not really, but it dawned on me I'd sicked it up and I shook more violent as I slid into the shallow water. I wondered if the pill had kicked in already or whether I really was screwed after all. I didn't even bother shampooing – I turned off the shower taps, then charged out of the bath and started drying myself furious with the stiff towel. For a second I considered taking the other pill on the windowsill, and I felt completely thick and confused while I hovered around. It was so shit, I couldn't even ask my mam for advice and I was torn between taking the risk or making a sad, mad rush to the health centre. I decided to head back down Overdale Road. There's that saying it's better to be safe not sorry, and it's better swallowing a pill than getting your life ruined. I swept all the water off myself then got changed into different clothes, pulling the lemon sweater over my head as I pressed down the stairs. Dave was washing oil off of spark-plugs or something in the kitchen, and at first he wanted to talk but I could hardly take it. His hands were covered in crap, and he came over and asked if I had a good night. 'Yeah, it was alright,' I replied; you could not tell the truth. I wondered what him or Mam would say if I came home with a baby. I had that weird feeling in my tum. I smiled slightly then grabbed at the pile of shoes by the door, slipping on my Ellesses again and yawning, 'I'm just popping out for some fags. You want anything?' Dave could tell I was only saying it; he shook his head and said, 'You seen Joe anywhere? Car's fucked again.' I shrugged — I hadn't seen my big bro for a while. He was usually out kicking footballs or courting lasses, but I wasn't in the mood to discuss it so I just waved and headed back out. I was still feeling queasy, shivering in the yellow jumper and not wanting to talk to anyone. It was ironic then that Shane, my boyfriend, appeared on the street corner. I was in sight of the health centre and everything, and all I could do was churn my belly and ask what he was up to. 'Just came up to see you. Can I come in?' Shane asked, and he kind of grabbed me and we drifted back the way I came. I glanced back at the centre with all its life-saving pills and other stuff, but I couldn't exactly say I got pregnant at a party and needed to get rid of it as soon as poss. I disguised a sigh as a normal breath, and we strode back into the house. I left Shane in the bedroom while I messed around in the lav – I decided to swallow the other pill just in case. Staring hard at the mirror, I still felt pretty dozy. In the end I managed to forget about it – me and Shane shagged later on in the day with the radio on and Sunday blowing in the window. And we remembered to put on a condom.

Baby Boy

Coochy coochy coo! My first brainwave was where the hell was I? There wasn't really much room to stretch your buds, but the pipes were full of Burger Kings and strawberry ice cream and it was pretty snug. I imagined coming out to yellow sand and blue skies and a big white palace. It wouldn't be that long. Every so often in the dark there was sunlight and a few different cocks probed around – it seemed like mammy was a bit of a slag. Gurgling, I kicked slightly then tried to sleep but she always put on Madonna when she was getting nailed, to drown out the sound of groaning probably. Hopefully when I got bigger no boys would want anything to do with her. I grinned and scoffed more draught cherry Coke. It was getting dead uncomfortable – I hoped these boys lying on top of her wouldn't shift me out of place and miscarry me. Life was going to be so big and exciting, all I could do was float around and wait for the day.

Chapter Seven

Horny Child

Eve

Friday morning was the first sign of it. She coughed up blood in the bathroom, just as I was psyching myself up for my mock exam. I'd been revising the night before, but Biology was really hard and I knew I'd go and lose it under pressure, plus you had the teachers prowling round you in silence like grim reapers. Why so much testing? In the bathroom I watched Mam wash away the red and black splashes with the taps on full-blast, and I felt down. She didn't want me to hug her because her chest hurt, but I had to. I had to stop shaking. Sniffing, I stood still for about ten minutes and I watched my watch ticking, making me late but I didn't care. I brushed my teeth while Mam pulled herself together, bent double over the cracked sink. She looked really sick, but I believed her when she said, Thanks, hun. I'm alright now.

I followed her out of the bathroom, then buckled up my school shoes at the top of the stairs, watching in case she collapsed on the way down. I had my Motorola phone ready for 999. But she never. Sitting in the carpet, I wanted to drag my sisters out of bed to keep an eye on her, but Natasha was at Dean's and Laura needed her beauty sleep before college in the afternoon. Mam was still pretty intent on going to work, and I grabbed my Warehouse bag and asked, Are you going to be okay?

Yeah, don't worry; it's happened before, she said, but you didn't want to hear that. Isn't it your Science test today?

I nodded as she handed me a pound for my dinner, and I pulled my Duffer top over my head while the sun plopped through the windows. It was startling. My crappy multiple-choice seemed so silly compared to Mam's bleeding lungs, but I cuddled her again and she said, Best of luck, love. I'm sure you'll do fine – I'll be thinking of you all day.

I prayed up to the sky she'd be alright. I glanced again at the heart-shaped watch, then had to quickly throw on my scarf and go for Jenni. Mam said good luck again as I kissed her goodbye, and outside in the freezy sunbeams it seemed horrible to leave her on her own like that. I watched kids and nutters walking round Keith Road at eight in the morning, and no one had a clue what we were going through. I didn't even tell Jenni about it – I went for her as normal and we waited for the school bus in total silence. For the whole day I felt bad that I hadn't told my mam I loved her, just in case. It was one of those days that went on for ever. Me and the girls arranged to go out, and with all the stress I was completely desperate to get mortalled. And in the end I felt like I screwed up the module test, but it wasn't the worst thing in the world. I wouldn't exactly need to know about peristalsis when I was a famous glamour model, or would I? I got home at about quarter to four after the bus was late and me and Dan got Anglo Bubbly at Easterside Bells, and I found out Mam hadn't made it into work after all. Apparently she sicked up a load more blood, drove herself to James Cook and had a ton of scans and blood tests and things. Me and Laura and Natasha were watching *Scooby Doo* when she came to sit between us, and you could tell she'd been crying. She told us that when you find lung cancer it's already past the point of getting it cured. Me and the girls suddenly sat up straight. It was too late to change our plans, but you felt like the biggest bitch in the world going out after news like that. And to cap it off I didn't even come home, instead sleeping with a boy named Johnny and doing a bottle of Hard. I tried to make it up to her the next night.

You're a star, Mam shouted as I boiled two cups of tea, but I didn't feel that special. I whizzed up the teas with two spoons, while Mam made herself comfy in the other room and got the TV on the right channel. We liked watching game shows and stuff on a Saturday night, although we didn't know many of the answers. Laura and Natasha had a weird way of dealing with bad news, and they went round munching a frozen pizza and waiting for phone calls. That night they were pretty downcast though. I juggled the full cups into the lounge, then bounced onto the sofa and gave Mam a huggle. At about 8:06 I got a text from Claire – she seemed a bit lonely, and she was asking if I was coming to the UGC or somewhere. She reckoned she'd split with Shane again over something or other, but I had too many lost souls to look after. In Year Nine me and Claire had a few daft slumber parties, and I remembered when she first started going with Shane and told me all about his dick and his positions and his noises. It was funny, and it was a little bit after that I started seeing Fairhurst.

Your tea okay? I asked Mam, but I knew all along I was the cup-of-tea queen. She nodded, then we messed with each other's hair once my phone finished vibrating. Mam was originally blonde like me, but she needed to dye again. Me and Laura only had a couple of years between us, and we had twin faces but her eyes and hair were a lot darker – I'd call it gerbil blonde. Natasha took after our dad, since she was taller and more Scandinavian-looking than all of us. I wanted to ask Mam if she'd told our dad about the cancer yet, but it was too tough to get the words out. He lived in South Bank with his new girlfriend, but she had nothing on his old one. Mam used to be pretty glamorous back when we were getting born – in old photos she looked like Diana Dors or someone like that, and I wondered if she ever did Page 3 or the sixties version of it. Debbie and Claire were always going on about modelling topless, and I imagined having that amazing lifestyle and getting out of Middlesbrough. I wondered what it'd be like going to all the crazy parties and snogging footballers or splitting up marriages. I laughed in my stupid head.

So how did your test go? Mam asked, and I wished she didn't remind me. My blonde hair fell back to earth, and I sighed on my chest.

Not so good, I replied, and left it at that. I wished some-times I could be clever as well as adorable – after all your brains last a lot longer than your face. In the end we turned off the quiz shows. We stared through a few adverts, then put on the *Sex and the City* DVD but none of us were in the mood for all that talk of willies and dildos though. Dean came round for a short while, and we considered going out to the Viking but the wind was yelling and I think Natasha wanted to go upstairs for a smooch instead. I couldn't face Natasha and Mam leaving Beechwood Avenue. I shivered a tiny tornado, picturing me and Laura getting orphaned like in *Oliver Twist* and moving to S/Bank. In all the commotion I started to feel sad, which wasn't like me – everything was going quite badly that day. I tried to focus on the TV set, hug my mam tighter, but it was a stupid weekend. Some people some places had pretty amazing lives, and they didn't even know it. I got up to make another cup of tea, but all I could do was swan around with stuff on my mind. The pink security light was blasting through the kitchen window, and as the water boiled I swivelled about in the colour. I could hear Dean and Natasha bouncing the bed upstairs, and Laura and Mam were laughing like idiots in the other room. At least they'd be around in the morning, and there was loads of time left to tell them I loved them. I felt myself tingle. We had a pretty amazing life and I knew it.

Adam

I was the boy who left home to learn fear. Instead of getting aggro at home for the loft wank, I wandered to Blockbuster where the Prick worked, stacking up boxes with him the next two nights, but it was fucking torture there and all. The videos got boring by six o'clock, and I made a sharp exit when the Prick went for a coffee in the back. Sometimes your friends aren't even that friendly, and the Prick was so boring I just couldn't waste my life flicking through Arnies or Rockys or even the X-rateds. He kept informing me which birds he'd love to put his knob up their bums. I felt crappy waiting for a bus back to Easterside, sitting alone at the top of a double-decker with the town getting ghostly around me. I'd started joining the Prick at Blockbuster after school-time, avoiding my parents but starving to death and just moping around dead depressed. I still hadn't seen Dad since I put my foot through the ceiling, and it was hard to gauge how cross everyone would be. I knitted my eyebrows all the way back to the estate, undoing my purple tie and hoping to god the night ahead would explode with happiness and lucky stars.

At Burny's they were all eating pepperoni pizzas, and I had to stand at the door until he was finished at the table. Eventually he came out with a glass of orange and vodka, glugging it while we talked and he nodded me in.

'You're early,' he said, but he wasn't holding it against me. I laughed nervously then kicked off my school shoes, feeling fucking stupid for being an awkward little devil.

'Yeah, well I haven't been home or nothing,' I said, scratching an eyelid. 'I've been up Blockbuster, but there's not much going on. What you been doing?'

'Nowt, just getting ready and all that.'

'Oh yeah, you haven't got a shirt I could lend?'

'Er, yeah, howay up,' Burny went, charging up the brown staircase. 'Donna's here and all.'

I tried to grin when we made it into his room, but it didn't come out right. Donna looked ace out of her Brackenhoe outfit, but she didn't really look at me and I felt myself slowly crawling back in my shell. Burny threw a plainish whiteish shirt at me then changed into a sky blue number himself, and occasionally I glanced at Donna who was undressing by the stretch mirror. She tugged off her red sweater without hesitating, then adjusted her boobs in a white bra and slipped on a shiny green halterneck thing. She had a load of different outfits round Burny's, and I gazed out the corner of my eye as she changed tops, swapped skirts, and twirled round to pieces of music. It was hornifying. Eventually Donna settled for the green, and I broke out of the trance and hurled on the white shirt in an embarrassed whirl. Burny poured a few cups of absinthe, and I swilled one straight down thinking it was only lime juice. I almost coughed my insides out, and I just nodded when he went, 'You ready? We might as well get going.'

It was my first night on the tiles. I left a bit of my school stuff on Burny's floor, then we slipped outside. Donna was kitted out in lizardy high-heels and a bag with her name on it, and it felt good walking around with a girl. I breathed my cheeks full of air, Burny and Donna yelled bye-byes to his family, and we set off into the night.

I shut the door gently four times then chased those two down Broadwell Road, where the dull semis bulged into terraces as the street swept out. Easterside had a fair amount of green space – unlike some other estates which were more cramped and jail-like – although you could still hear the sounds of rogues and screaming girls on the wishy-washy wind. I sniffed up that freezing smell of the night, and a shiver went down my back as the streetlights spun our shadows round and round while we stepped forward. There were knots in my belly about getting into the pub, but there was also some excitement there somewhere and a sexy little feeling in my long-johns.

'Cheers for bringing me out,' I murmured, once Burny and Donna stopped swinging and kissing each other. Occasionally couples were annoying, but only when you're not in one. I caught them up again as we crossed over, and Burny said, 'It's alright. We'll get dead wrecked.'

'Have you brought lots of money?' Donna asked, with a glinty look in her eyes.

'Eh, about fifteen,' I replied, cars bouncing over speed-bumps at our sides. I was the dictionary definition of a gooseberry.

'You looking forward to tonight?' I asked her, but she couldn't be bothered answering. The Grove was smarter than the Viking, though it had to be done up every time it got torched. It was busier than I imagined but Burny burrowed to the bar, his arms round Donna's waist like she was a shiny shield. All I got was stares and a brick of paranoia. Often these places were like the OK Corral, except the cowboys in Middlesbrough were all on steroids and dressed in Sherman and trackies. I wasn't sure what I wanted to drink, so I asked for whatever Burny was having when he got the first round. Me and Donna went into the corner and got some stools by the pool-table, and I found it really hard to say anything to her. We ended up talking about the carpet and the sound-system, and it was a big relief when the drinks came over. I managed to loosen up though the getting drunk part was lined with a feeling of being lonely and bored. Me and Burny had a conversation while pool-balls clattered, but sometimes him and Donna had to go kiss and whisper sweet-nothings, and I felt shitty. I glanced at sexy groups of girls getting pissed, but how the hell were you supposed to go up to them? They were all rowdy bints getting chatted up by blockheads. After a bit more sitting it was my turn to get some drinks, and I paced across the room trying not to bump into anyone. I spotted Dan Williams in the corner with all these wide-boys he knew from school, but we never really talked to each other so I pretended not to see him. Waiting at the bar my tummy was stuttering and I felt panicky, but what an anticlimax – I was expecting to get chucked on the street by bouncers in bomber-jackets for being fifteen years old, but the barmaid just smiled and squirted my pints of lager. She looked about twenty or thirty with dark frazzled hair, and I grinned back but she didn't fancy me or anything. It was nice to get some bit of recognition though, and walking back to the pool-balls I started feeling better and kept my eyes peeled for anyone I could get my hands on.

When I used to live in Saltersgill there was a girl who rode past my house every morning on a pink bike, and though she was engraved in my head as a six-year-old it was funny seeing her standing there by the snooker table. She was about seventeen now, and I was hoping just to slink past and mind my own business but she grabbed me and went, 'Is that Adam thingy?' I nodded, luckily not throwing the pints all over her. We talked for a bit about shit stuff like Saltersgill Avenue and pints of lagers, and since my hands were full of glasses I wasn't doing all that nervous body-language like scratching my face and cross-ing my arms and biting my nails. I actually thought I was getting somewhere until she snapped, 'Anyways, gotta go. I'm meeting me boyfriend at Aruba.'

Back at the table, Burny and Donna were dead embar-rassing and asking about the girl but I wasn't a wanker so I kept my mouth shut. For some reason it was a macho thing in Boro to say, 'Would've nailed her, fucking dirty slag.' But I'd be lucky. The girls I went for all had blonde hair and blue eyes, not that I was Hitler; it was probably the purity and innocence that got me going. Having said that, lasses with those attributes like Eve or Rachel or Claire Blame were always going out and getting into mischief while a normal night for me was getting tucked up in bed by half-ten. So I necked the next pint a bit quicker, not really enjoying it, and I got the kick to get up and wander around again. There were quite a few pretty faces, but I didn't know how to act and when an Aryan bombshell brushed past me I had a cheeky little feel of her sides. God knows what I would've done if she turned around. I had no chat-up lines or come-hither expressions. In actual fact I got clocked by her boyfriend, who was trailing behind with arms the size of beer barrels. Straight away I shit myself, and he sort of barged into me and snarled, 'Watch out then you fucking prick.' All I could think about was Pablo Picasso – everything about her boyfriend was dead square and cubist. Hideous.

So from then on I decided not to be so forward and sleazy, although if a square cunt like him could get a beauty then so could anyone. I chose a spot at the bar next to these two brunettes, one of them much better-looking than the other but they both had on nice summery dresses and they shone out on such a frosty night. While I waited to get served I eavesdropped, and when Summer Girl 1 asked Summer Girl 2 for the time I took a stab in the dark and went, 'About nineish,' and smiled. They looked at me doss-eyed and I figured they were both sloshed, so I pouted all stupid and asked, 'What are you drinking, ladies?' They just laughed though.

Burny and Donna were still watching me from the corner, and I felt daft staggering back to the chairs but who gives a fuck – the beer and a half had kicked in, and I was having a good time I think. I plonked back down on the seat, but we still couldn't really say anything to each other and I figured they wouldn't ask me out again. The Grove was beginning to empty and these other girls came over to sit at the table next to us, and as I slurped the new Carlsberg the confidence wobbled back again. I sat with my legs slightly open on the off-chance one of them moved up against me, but there was no joy. They yapped on like puppy dogs, all sorts of things like how men are total pigs and dickheads and I decided to take my leg back. After a bit we had to finish those drinks and we dragged ourselves outdoors, and I'd almost forgotten the shit estate was out there. We tackled it together.

Donna was the last girl standing in the swirling night. She was pissing herself between me and Burny but it was sweet, and I held her sides and she felt like toasted marshmallow. She brightened me up with a cherry on top. I asked if there was any chance I could come back and sleep at theirs, but I knew they'd want to make babies and stuff and I had to go back home sooner or later. My parents would be in bed, and hopefully I could creep in without having to shut the door too many times. I dreaded bumping into them though, now they knew I was a complete wanker. After a firm no from the lovebirds, I sighed the goodbyes and started charging home as the cold set in. Donna at least sent me off with a peck on the cheek, but as soon as they disappeared I was left with the same crap feeling and I wondered to myself how was I ever going to avoid another beating.

Chapter Eight

Outside Is OK

Eve

I bought the yellow Hello Kitty beanie for five pound, but I knew I wouldn't wear it and in the end I gave it to Mam when her hair started falling out. Me, Debbie and Rachel swung our shopping bags as we flounced out of the Hill Street Centre, all of us really jolly compared to the dour grey faces trundling round Boro that afternoon. The town seemed to be a beautiful playground, all the silver factories and pipes and flares sticking up over the little strawberry rooftops, and we bounced around like three-year-olds on Prozac. The weather was good, and we got our holiday booked. Claire was at home with flu or something, but the four of us were jet-setting to Majorca the following March – it was only some off-season resort, but we figured it was worth it what with GCSEs coming up and also the crap spring wind and rain. As we stepped onto Linthorpe Road and saw everyone going about in their drab outfits and sour expressions, we stuck our eyes on the sun and imagined what it would be like.

Where next? Debbie asked us, squinting a little. We weren't ones to float around in posh sunglasses, but then again I believed all the stuff about getting crow's feet. Rachel pushed up her sexy sixties shades while me and

Debbie screwed our faces up, and even though she was seeing everything in black and brown she was the first to say, Look, there's Gary.

Gary Clinton was the biggest gangster in Brackenhoe school. We'd scored a few love-heart pills from him the night before, and we were wandering around with that dreamy Happy Monday feeling in our heads except it was Saturday. Everything seemed funny and beautiful. Gary was also the type of boy to go round smacking kids from other schools, and trying to shag girls who didn't know any better. I was pretty sure he hadn't nailed any of my gang – I personally wouldn't go anywhere near him, even though he was charming when he was trying to get into you. He had on an eighties-looking black and green shellsuit, and did the upward nod when he spotted us coming over. He thought he was the king of cool, and me and Rachel had a tiny smirk about it with linked arms.

Alright? he asked once we reached him. What youse up to?

Nowt; we just booked our hol to Majorca, I explained. I breathed in when he looked at my tits.

Mint. Any decent clubs out there like, or what?

Well yeah, it's got Pacha and everything, Rachel replied, but Gary didn't have a clue. All he knew about was nutting and glassing people in Time and Bongo. He had a silly life.

So what you doing? I asked him, but I wasn't as interested as that.

Gaz blinked up and down the rainbow-dotted street, then went, Tried to get some money off this lad. I dunno now. I was gonna nick some bottles or something. Youse need owt getting?

God did he know what women wanted. Rachel and me

just laughed, but you could see the cogs ticking in Debbie's head and she went, Some spraypaint?

It was fair enough not wanting to spend three or four pound on a can of paint, but it meant Gaz had to hang around with us the rest of the day and you couldn't talk about the stuff you wanted to with him around. Gary shrugged black/green sheeny shoulders, then those two went off to find a car shop. Me and Rachel waited out in the sun while they scooted in and stole plum, lime green and raspberry red, and later on we spotted them getting off on the benches near Virgin. I guessed it was payback for the paint – a kiss from Debbie had a street-value of about twenty-five pound. Even back then Deb was seeing darkie Brandon from North Ormesby – Gary didn't have any colour to him whatsoever. Me and Rachel got a couple of pasties out of Greggs, but we could hardly stomach anything having been on the love-hearts the previous evening. We just stood and played about with the pastry – in a way ecstasy was a good way to keep your figure. If you gave E to completely fat people not only would they be buzzing all the time, the weight would topple off them. Debbie was jiggling her knees while Gaz felt her up – they were getting into it, but you could hardly watch. Me and Rach laughed but they were a nuisance – once they prised themselves off each other, Debbie and Gary lagged behind the rest of the day and in a weird way you hoped Brandon would appear round the corner with a bomby-knocker.

Gary had a foil-lined carrier out with him – I seriously wondered if he was for real, spending Saturday afternoons stealing things and putting fingers up girls' rude bits. In broad daylight as well. It was a gorgeous day – I tried not to worry too much but he was mental, and I strode forwards chatting with Rach. We got loads of looks off boys as we rocketed up the pavement, but we were in the mood for just staring straight ahead like stuck-up supermodels. Every now and then we had to say hello to people we were associated with. On the corner of Vaughan Street, Gary wanted to browse in JD Sports, and yet again me and Rachel giggled about his class although we had been known to wear Fila and Adidas and Kappa and Ellesse back in the day. Actually I woke up in trackie bottoms that morning but let's keep that one to ourselves. Rach came back to mine after a night down the Viking, and we changed into comfy clothes and watched the last of the Friday telly. The lovehearts especially tended to give you that speedy up-all-night effect, so we were there on the settee til about five or six in the morning, wired to it.

It's boiling, Rachel said, taking off her shades as we pushed through everyone in the tight shop. It was the perfect scenario for swiping sportswear, but you just could not look. Me and Rach dragged Debbie over to the swimwear and stroked a few bikinis, trying not to be seen with Gaz. Debbie was neither here nor there, but all the talk of holidays got her in the mood again and we nattered a while about beaches and Sex On The Beaches. There was better fun to come than hanging around with scallywags. We watched Gary smuggle away a pair of sky blue Kappa trackies, and after a bit it was obvious the security guard was going to get involved. I had a hold on a red Adidas bikini top when the hunky guy in black marched over, but Gaz spotted him pretty fast and burst his way out. The trackies were hanging out the foil bag when he crossed the alarm but it didn't go off, and Debbie shoved her bum in the security man's side and he had no choice but to manhandle her.

Watch out then! What the fuck you doing, Debbie said, and for a second she fazed him with her bedtime eyes and pneumatic breasts. I almost laughed, but Rachel was staring the opposite way and instead we decided to watch Gaz sprint off. The guard got all flustered, made a charge for the door then changed his mind and said to us, Do you know that lad?

Naw but I'd like to get to know you, Deb said, and we left it at that. The security guard was sort of cute, and obviously he was too hot and bothered to put up a chase. Instead we spotted him talking to his walkie-talkie as we walked the other way, and I wondered who was on the other end. To be honest with you I didn't care if Gaz got caught or not – it was a relief to get rid of him the rest of the afternoon. I touched the Lunn Polly papers in my jeans then smoothed out my yellow cotton top, and me and the girls started waltzing off.

Adam

I finally woke up in my own bed. My brain was all misty from My First Hangover, and then it got pummelled in by my dad. It turned out my parents weren't happy I'd run away. After the massive argument I got grounded and pounded, and forced to watch the TV set with them. Alone in my room god knows what lewd acts I'd get up to. In actual fact I only wanted to go and put on *Rubber Soul*, but instead of levitating to George's sitar I had to sit there in front of *Stars in Their Eyes*. I couldn't manage the lotus position, but I was seeing stars though. It was weird over breakfast my dad saying I could've been murdered, then proceeding to smack me round the face. I'd only been away a couple of days, but he kicked me all round the kitchen – it was sort of my fault falling into the corner of the cooker though. I had a bit of a black eye again, and watching Matthew Kelly was quite slitty and painful.

My dad was weird, but he wasn't all that bad – don't be thinking he was child-abusing me, after all I was fifteen years old. He was always going on about his hectic life, working at British Steel and then coming home to a stupid tosser like me. He'd been working on the plant for about twenty years, and with all that pollution and dust in his system perhaps he'd gone clinically insane. We used to do all sorts together like seeing films, kicking footies and driving about, but nowadays we could hardly look at each other and I supposed he wanted a big butch son not a pervert with the OCD.

'Can you pass us a mint, love?' my mum asked. I had to shut the tin a couple of times or else she'd choke on it. Mum was always chewing mints since she was chaining Mayfairs so much, and slowly the smoking had contorted her face into a mountain-face. Maybe that's why my dad was going mad all the time – his wife was getting quite horrible, but at least he had someone to love. I didn't have that reassurance yet that I wouldn't be dying alone in some Easterside flat, and it was scary. That night at the Grove mixed me up – I couldn't see myself with any of the girls in there, and at school I wasn't exactly Casanova neither. It didn't make a difference – that evening over fish-finger sarnies my parents decided to suspend my pocket money, which was only five pound but still though.

'Just going to the toilet,' I said, getting up. I had to slam the bathroom door four times, and I'm surprised they didn't shout at me or follow me up. The having to shut things all the time was starting to grate on me – everything to me seemed like a Pandora's Box, as if leaving something slightly ajar would launch a thousand scares and nightmares into the big bad world. I was always paranoid. I sighed on the toilet seat, and I felt like an absolute daft cunt. Just to avoid my parents for a bit, I sat looking at the circles on the wallpaper and wondered if to spite them I should wank all over the place. I hated them. Firework night was the worst, about a month down the line, staying in watching *Corrie* while all the bangs went off outside. It must've been a Friday because Dad was at the Beechwood Easterside, and sitting in with my mum was soul-destroying. I had to sit with my head down while she puff-puffed, though in the corner of your eye you could catch odd sparky colour outside and shit yourself at all the booms.

'Ooh, did you hear that one,' was all she could say. Of course you did – it was blitzkrieg, and I wanted to be out there. Mum was a lot more amiable than my dad, but she was dead boring and she always went along with whatever he said. How are your kids meant to go anywhere in life if you just ground them all the time? All I could do was sit around staring at walls, fantasising about bonfires and Catherine wheels and sparkles. Funnily enough Burny hadn't invited me out since we went down the Grove, but there was the Christmas disco on its way and I figured we'd hook up for that. In the past I never bothered with the discos and suchlike, too scared about dancing or fighting or being embarrassing but I saw it as a good excuse for them to let me out again.

'That was a loud one,' Mum said, these red stars dropping round the rooftops. There was a bonfire down Saltersgill field, and I had in my head all the fun going on underneath the light show. And in contrast the sheer hell staring at the Rover's Return on telly. It was the nearest I'd been to a pint of lager since for ever. Dad had started keeping his bedroom in strict order, so now there was no chance finding a bottle of booze or porno mag or anything – it was just wall-to-wall boredom. Mum worked at Greggs in the Village and she often brought home pastries and whatnot, but sitting in stuffing your face was pretty miserable too. I crunched into a chicken bake, wallowing in pain and eating it so slowly on purpose.

'God I nearly had a heart attack!' the stupid cow said. I didn't speak. We watched a really beautiful one – it was gold and exploded into five bits, and those bits exploded into five bits, and so did those bits. I tried to make a wish, and it had something to do with girls and discos and stuff like that. I carried on the stubborn act for the rest of November.

Chapter Nine

Doggy

Eve

When Natasha had her hen night I wore the mauve dress and the appropriate shoes, these little purple fellows with the fake Jimmy Choo logo. We pushed through the peeling doors of the Social, then strode to the set of tables they'd cordoned off for our party and plonked down. Me, Natasha, Laura and Mam were all dressed to kill. It was ages since we'd all been somewhere, and Mam was more than willing to get us pissed on her dinnerlady wages. We swanned about in different colours: me purple, Natasha in silver, Laura peachy-orange, and Mam in a new black number. I learnt in English no words rhyme with purple, silver or orange, but it didn't spoil it. There were tons of Natasha's friends already sat at the table, and I knew it would be fun times when they started cackling and howling as we all downed drinks. Mam didn't want me going too mad because it was a school night, but as soon as she got tipsy she was practically forcing the drinks down my neck.

Stripper's coming at half-eight, then we've got taxis for Time at tenish, one of Natasha's mates said to her; I didn't recognise all of them, but it was nice to see loads of people there. I guessed a lot of the girls had been to school with her, or worked with her in the pound shop or One-Stop or the Top Shop. I wasn't sure if I was allowed to invite Debbie or Rachel or Jen or anyone like that, but I liked the idea of spending the night with just my family. I wasn't sure who invited the old men in the corner, though; they looked identical in brown and grey workshirts, slurping beers and black lagers while their eyes popped out at us. Natasha had a mission for the hen night (1 = get ten guys' phone numbers, 2 = blow up ten guys' condoms), but she'd get nowhere in here. The place smelled a little bit like vasectomies.

Drinks were only about a pound, and we gradually got sillier as the karaoke machine spun the colour lights. A few girls I didn't know and one of our cousins from our dad's side got up to wail a few songs, but most of the night me and Laura just sat and whispered to each other and kept well out of it. Mam and her dinnerlady pals had done the buffet, and some of the old blokes tried to tax it while we tucked into the ham buns and those tiny sausage rolls and cheese-on-sticks. It was gorgeous, and I was famished. My head was light as air and I felt embarrassed for the men trying to flirt with us in the blacklight. I had all my defences down and my mouth full.

Nice to see some young ladies in here for once, one of them said to me; he was about fifty with scruffy hair and almost a full beard. I smiled, then moved away discreetly but he added, So youse are staying all night?

Naw, I don't know, I replied, but I could've just said we were going to Time.

So do you have a fella then? the guy carried on, gobbling up a few Pringles.

No, I snapped. I looked him in the eye and took a bite of a chipolata, then added, I'm only thirteen.

I thought that'd scare him off, but he sort of chuckled and went, Well that's alright by me. Maybe you come and sit on my knee later on?

I blinked and toddled off. I hoped to the Lord he was joking. Back in the corner we had more Archers and Cokes on the table, and we scoffed loads and drank ourselves to bits while a stripper jigged about. He was supposed to be a fireman but he didn't have the scorch marks. I kept out of trouble by sitting between Mam and Laura – a few girls on the other side of the table got writhed against and got bits of uniform round their necks. I just laughed. Natasha naturally had to rub baby oil into the stripper and squirt squirty-cream on his tail – he had an amazing job really. Everyone was shrieking and I got blurry eyes from all the joy and drinks. When the stripper finished his routine he knocked around for a couple lagers – he was from either Berwick Hills or Pallister, and Natasha got his phone number for her mission thing. I was feeling extremely pissed by nine o'clock, and me and Mam ended up rambling about boys and school stuff while everyone went all over the place. Waking up in the morning was going to be disgraceful.

The main thing is just enjoy your life, Mam said to me, and I cringed but she was dead right. You should definitely try to be happy all the time while you're on this earth. I clapped my heels on the lino floor and pulled down my mauve top. While she talked she patted my hand, and I spotted the beardy paedo still staring at us across the brown room. The old blokes got ushered back in when the stripper finished, and I was surprised they were still interested in sex after that. I rolled my eyes up to the ceiling and tried not to look at them.

You okay, honey? Mam asked, rubbing a finger up her glass. I stabbed her with eyelashes, then went, Are you coming to Time with us? I just wanna get going, you know what I mean.

Mmm, yeah it should be fun, she replied. She was looking really well with her face made up and the fifties black-and-white hat – it was one of those nights you prayed you don't get a maudlin-mouth and talk about the cancer.

I sat up in my chair then downed the rest of an Archers, wobbly as anything and looking forward to grooving at the club. I tried to think which boys would be out, but I hadn't asked around – I thought about texting someone, but I was so pissed it didn't really matter who I got off with. Before the minibuses, Natasha had to do a speech about not getting to fuck any other boys but Dean and having to clean up after him when they moved to Gresham, then Mam roped me, Laura and Natasha into singing 'Like a Virgin' together on the karaoke. I wondered if Mam thought we were still virgins, but we belted it out anyhow. Back in the day we'd all pretended to be Madonna in our rooms at least once – I wasn't much of a singer, but I posed like a starlet as the ball thing bounced along the words. I didn't look the way of the old men, but you could catch them all applauding as we came off the stage. It was a bit of a relief when the Boro Taxis started tooting their horns outside. We piled in and shot up Marton Road like randy girls on a hen night, me and Laura and Natasha and Mam and a few cousins and a few of Natasha's mates squeezed in one, everyone else in the other. I held on for dear life as the bus swerved and bobbled my head around. I pushed the frilly boob bits off my shoulders, watching the town fly by as the driver put his foot down. I was feeling frosty, but I rocked around in a haze of Archers and tried not to keel over. When we got to Time we had to wait outside for the other minibus to catch up, and me and Laura and Mam huddled in a cuddle while Natasha chattered to her mates on the roadside. Someone had given her a banner saying DON'T TOUCH: I'M ENGAGED but she wasn't looking too dishevelled yet in her chainmail dress – I was just happy there was no way she could get stabbed that night.

We got into Time at about ten o'clock, and Natasha swanned around with her best mates trying to conjure up phone numbers and plastic johnnies. Laura met up with a few boys from St Mary's, dancing with them in the centre of the room and probably getting a few gropes. They weren't bad looking actually. Me and Mam watched from the side of the dancefloor, spending the whole night together and getting bored a lot quicker than everyone else. I didn't want to be the one to ditch her, but it was miles too loud to talk to each other and we couldn't exactly go on the pull. Mam never wanted to hook up with anyone after our dad, especially after she found out about the cancer. With the drinks fading off, the hen night began to feel incredibly rubbish. Drained by boredom and old pervs trying to cop off with me, I didn't want to socialise and me and Mam ended up getting a taxi home an hour after getting in. After all it was a school night, and the thought of my yellow ducks bedcover was starting to feel like heaven. I set my mind on that and we set off into the night. And I made sure I didn't say one thing about the cancer.

Debbie

.sdrawkcab no erew stnap sih yllatnediccA .esuoh eht morf yawa klaw mih gnihctaw das tlef I dna ,wodniw ym tuo dekool I .sregilliH sih tsuj ni edistuo nworht gnitteg ekil t'ndid eh ylsuoivbo – niaga denohp reven dna deracs tog baF .ti detah dad ym teb I .llew sa elyts yggod gniod erew ew dna tuo gnippop bonk sih fo pals tew eht – em ffo baF gnillup dad ym fo dnuos eht tegrof reven ll'I .thgin ta eman ym gniyarps dna meht gnisahc syad ym tneps I dna ,syob kcalb rof etats eht dah I no neht morF .kliM yriaD s'yrubdaC ekil dekool dna teews saw eh tub ,taht retfa hcum rehto hcae ees t'ndid ew – hguoht ,baF devol I .yeknom a yb nepo tilps gnitteg rethguad sih was eh nehw rorroh eht enigami dna moordeb ym otni demrots eh, gnikcinaP .rehtegot owt dna owt tup t'ndluoc eh – ylthgils gnikaeuqs deb eht dna gninaorg dna gninaom em draeh eh nehw eew a rof gniog saw eH .deredrum gnitteg saw I thguoht ev'tsum dad yM .niap fo tib ysneet a htiw gnikeirhs dna gninihw neht dna won pleh t'ndluoc I tub ,mhtyhr pets-owt a pu dekrow eh elihw mih kcen dna ecaf s'baF barg ot deirt I – decneirepxeni mees ot tnaw t'ndid I .sni- girv htiw yaw eht syawla taht t'nsi – gnits gniht sih tlef I dna pu dehcnum tog steehsdeb der yM .seilliw gib gnivah skcalb tuoba eurt demees ti tub ot ti erapmoc ot hcum evah yllaer t'ndid I .ni ti kcuts eh dna em fo pot no lwarc mih tel I ,dnuora gniporg dna gnissik fo tib elttil a retfA .sretsop idnoD eht derimda eh kniht I tub ,deb ym no tas ew sa teiuq ytterp erew eW .trap nigriv eht tuoba mih llet t'ndid

I .neethgie saw I mih dlot I − ytinigriv ym esol ot tuoba
saw I dna eno-ytnewt saw baF esuaceb deticxe daed gnitteg
saw I edisplif eht nO .gnihtemos detuohs dna su was enoe-
mos esac ni suovren tlef llits I tub ,tuoba eno on saw ereht
− daoR llewdaorB nwod deklaw ew sa sdnah dleh baF dna
eM .sgowillog meht dellac syawla dad yM .rehtona ot led
gniht eno yllarutan dna etatse eht ot kcab ixat a derahs su fo
ruof eht dna ,eohnekcarB morf lad dnolb emos dellup dah
evE .ffo dekcik yletelpmoc dad ym ,edisretsaE ot kcab dal a
thguorb I emit tsrif ehT .tnagorra lla dnuora tnew llits
syoB-B eht tub ,decidujerp daed eb dluoc oroB ni elpoep
esuaceb sredistuo ekil tlef llits syug eseht fi derednow I .spil
kcalb evissam rieht no pu dne dna meht tsniaga pu bur ot
ysae ytterp saw ti sdneirflrig evah t'ndid yeht fI .dnuora
gnippob syoB-B eht gnihctaw dna ehcarae gnitteg srekaeps
eht yb emit elohw eht tneps I dna yadsruhT eno
esuohrenroC eht ot tnew won ot klat t'nod ew srehto wef
a dna evE dna em ,eniN raeY retfa remmus tuoba nI .syob
kcalb eht yltsom saw ti :yaw eht ni tog taht aixelsyd eht
yllaer t'nsaw ti uoy htiw tsenoh eb oT .eibbeD tleps yllaer
saw ti knew I ;hgual a rof taht ekil ti etorw ylno I − yggoD
nwod EDIS/E VO EBED hctarcs ot nwonk neeb dah I
.dnuorgyalp ybsemrO htroN nwod selbbircs esoht edtnuoc
uoy sselnu ,enecs farg a evah yllaer t'ndid hguorbselddiM
.erucinam ruoy dekcerw elzzird tniap eht dna ,hguoht pu
ezorf sregnif ruoy semitemoS .selbbub dna wobniar fo lluf
llaw a ot thgilyad daorb ni kcab gnimoc neht ,srettel eht tuo
triuqs uoy elihw flesruoy gnippap − elbidercni saw hsur
ehT .pu eman ym tup dna revlis dna knip toh fo nac a htiw
tuo tnew I thgin taht ,trohs yrots gnol a tuc ot oS .efil ni
erehwyna teg ot gniog saw I fi evitaerc eb ot dah I wenk I

aixelsyd eht tuoba tuo dnuof I nehW .trap ytra eht htiw
thgirla saw eh tub ,deretrauq dna nward gnuh dna derehtaef
dna derrat tog elpoep kcalb erehw emit a ni pu werg dad
ym esoppus I .ecilop morf yawa gninnur dna stnulb
,sruoloc thgirb – gnizama os dekool efil taht dna ,(syob itiffarg etiruovaf ym lla) sretsop senoniuQ eeL dna edalB and
idnoD yb dednuorrus moor ym ni gnittis rebmemer I
.ecnassianeR eht ekil saw ti itiffarg derevocsid I nehw tub
,loohcs morf etS dna zaG dna naD ekil elpoep ycnaf ot desu
I – gnirob dna ykeeg tib a demees syob etihw em oT
.sadidA orter dna sorfA htiw yseehc tib elttil a fi ,suoegrog
erew seithgie eht ni CYN ni detniap ohw sepyt yoB-B eht
– setsac-flah dna skcalb otni neeb syawla d'I .gnilleps naht
wolf dna sruoloc tuoba erom saw ti tub ,sdrow gnitirw
tuoba lla gnieb ti htiw itiffarg otni tog I driew s'tI .sdrawk-
cab nwod sgniht deipoc I yllatnediccA

Chapter Ten

3 Children on a Dancefloor

Eve

Downstairs was a mountain of condoms. I never got the chance to ask Natasha how the mission went – I just cracked up and carried on getting ready with the TV talking to me. I think it was *Newsround*. I wasn't overly keen on these school disco things – often it was just an excuse for the geeks to come out and pretend to be wild, but it was Christmas and the only way to have fun on a Tuesday night really. I put on a load of Urban Decay and sipped up some vodka but I didn't want to go too mad; all the teachers would be there and I didn't want them seeing me in a predicament. The rest of the girls were upstairs – the disco was fancy dress, and we made a pact to come out looking like cats. I had on Mam's black dress with the one-inch sleeves, a white belt from H+M with a cat's tail attached to the back. We got the tails from a shop off Borough Road, and we painted three sexy whiskers on each cheek and went round and round our eyes with mascara. I had on sheer black gloves up to my elbows and Laura's shin-high black booties – some of the girls had on cuffs and collars like playboy bunnies, and when I stepped into my bedroom again I laughed. Surprise surprise Debbie was a brown kitten, Gracie had gone for white albino stylee and

Claire was looking really pregnant under her tight tabby outfit. Rachel and Jenni were similar to me in simple black and white – we were all bums and boobs and paws, the outfits clung to you like anything. We had a few cheap bottles of wine flowing while we got ready, Radio One chirping in the background but it was just the indie crap they put on weeknights. We were all crouched round my bedside mirror, pissing ourselves because we looked like total freaks. Me, Claire and Rachel purred at each other while we sat on my yellow duvet, preening ourselves. Perhaps it was the drink but the night felt unstoppable – it was a bit like prom night with all of us crammed in the one room. There was that slight expectation that the music and the disco was going to be shite, but the fact we were dressed as cats gave it that extra kick. Mam kept coming in with the Kodak.

Are youse going to be warm enough? she asked, standing in the doorframe. She had a constant beaming grin like she'd taped her face up, and it set us off. I ran the fuzzy black tail through my fingers, then snorted and said, Yeah it's not that far. Should be a good laugh walking down.

We've got a layer of fur and all that, Debbie added, her always being quick off the draw with corny little gags.

There were purrs and miaows of agreement, then we carried on making ourselves up as Mam headed off. I gassed us all with hairspray then put on the Burberry Brit. I let Claire borrow some Urban Decay – none of us talked to her about the baby; it was hard to tell if she wanted it or not, and we didn't want to put any kind of downer on Claire's night. It was worrying to think that in a month or two she wouldn't be able to go out at all, or come to school, but you couldn't just say get an abortion because I know from watching TV it's not as simple as that.

Can you pass us the Bella? Debbie asked me, grabbing for the wine. Her eyes were already a little glazed from the drink and I giggled, staring each other out with our daft kitten faces. Her fake tan was caked on like black-face make-up, and it looked obscure with her hair braided. I took a big gulp, Bellabrusco being the tastiest of all the wines, then pretended to hide it under my tail before passing it over. Debbie sniggered then took a long swig and came out with, You tight pussy.

That put us in stitches and we laughed and cried for about ten hours. I had to hold my sides and a lot of Bella got spat across the carpet and sheets. We calmed down after a bit. I tried to mop up some of the mess with a few Kleenex, but the carpet was dingy anyway and I wasn't that fussed. It was seven o'clock and we were just about ready. We licked our paws, checked the make-up again, then started to head downstairs. I made sure my bag was full of crap, and we scampered out one by one with our ears pricked up.

Right, see you later Mam, I shouted into the living room. We won't be too late.

Okay, have a good time lovey, Mam said back, then there was a little confusion with everyone shouting bye-byes at the same time and mewing like knobheads. We chuckled out of the door. It felt weird being out on the spooky streets all of a sudden, dressed as fucking kittens while everyone else went about their business. We padded across tracing-paper frost, all the Crimbo lights illuminating the nutcases like a festive Chamber of Horrors. Some gardens had massive plastic

Santas, reindeer and whizzing fairylights, and I loved the over-the-topness of the estate. Christmas would be marvellous. We got a few cat calls as we marched down the rest of Keith Road and crossed to Belle Vue Convenience, but all you could do was fall about laughing because we were in such good spirits. We weren't dead nervous getting served at Belle Vue any more, but we sent in Debbie and Gracie anyway because they had the large boobs. I followed them in just for the fun of it – we turned a few heads. I made feline moves around the aisles while Grace and Debbie picked up six-packs of Smirnoff Ice and Castaway – a few oldish men were staring over, and a bunch of kids at the sweety section were trying to take the piss but let's face it they were all wanking their willies over us.

How old are youse? the assistant asked Debbie when they brought the bottles to the counter, but she was smirking at the same time.

Nineteen, she replied, then she pulled a face as if to say: can you believe we're nineteen and we still dress up like cats. The assistant bagged up the drinks and Deb and Gracie paid with a twenty. We all chipped in except for Claire, who was being a good mummy and not drinking or smoking til the baby popped out. I was actually starting to yearn for a pill and all, but I swear to god if I told one the teachers I loved them I wouldn't come into school again.

Where are you going tonight? the assistant asked, handing over the change. I straightened my Mickey Mouse ears then came over to the girls and butted in, It's our work do. Fancy dress and that.

You don't say, the assistant went, and she laughed as we catwalked out. It was slightly chilly as we stood about and cracked open the drinks on sides of walls – we ended up huddling under the bus shelter while cars beeped past us. The darkness was huge all around, and we got more and more pissed as we shivered and chittered. Rach, Debbie and Gracie squashed up on the red plastic bench, passing round Castaways while Claire began to look bored. I stayed with her and let her slurp some alcopop while the 63 and 27A went past, with a few depressed-looking youngsters sat on the back. I started to imagine us sitting about in Majorca – it would be amazing to get out of the frost, and the streets would be paved with Spanish studs. I didn't like rubbing it in though, since Jenni and Gracie weren't joining us and they always seemed to suck a lemon whenever it got mentioned. At the time they said they were too skint to go all the way to the Balearics, but I couldn't stomach another trip to Blackpool or Scarborough. We often got laid at the seaside, but it just wasn't the same.

There'd better be a few others in fancy dress, I said, gazing over my bottle at the middle of the road. We got on the next 27, finishing off the Smirnoff Ices as we rattled down Marton Road. The driver thought it was good crack having a bunch of pussycats on his bus on such a miserable night, and he stared down our tops while we paid up some change.

Well I think Tyler's going as Elvis, Debbie said as me and her perched on the set of eight seats near the back. We bounced around as we set off, trying to check our hair and outfits in the windows which were all bright and reflective. Tyler was this lad from Debbie's Science class and, although he was quite dashing, I couldn't really see him as the King. He was skinny, with a skinhead.

Miaow thank you, I giggled as we jumped off the bus a

few stops later. It felt weird going back to school in the middle of the night, all the lights still on and the teachers in casual clothes. People like Mr Barley always seemed to go for really twatty jeans and stuff like that. We slipped by without saying hello.

It was stifling when we got in the hall, and suddenly all the boys' faces caught ours and we went on the prowl. We were all smiley and drunk, and the daft little disco lights were going though there was no one really dancing. Luckily we had enough alcopop inside us to start swishing our tails into the centre of the hall, and we marked our territory. There were a few people dressed as nurses and gangsters and Miss Santa Clauses and a few goths were vampires, but me and the girls looked the business. We danced in a looseish circle, me staring and pretending to flirt with brown Debbie on the opposite side. We threw our handbags down for the sake of it. It was just tacky old pop music and the DJ was only there to gaze at the girls, but we hot-stepped to and fro like something out of *Top Cat*. It was slightly funny and slightly boring – thank god we had drinks. Rach and Debbie smuggled a few Castaways in their bags, and we spent the night popping to the loo and keeping the good times going. Some hip-hop stuff brought a few lads onto the dancefloor but they were all shit dancers, keeping their arms by their sides while they jigged about on the spot. Gaz came up behind me and gave me a manhandle – I pretended to be pleased to see him. He looked extremely wasted – you could tell he was on drugs by the way he wibbled about and stared mad eyes at you. He was sweaty and kept looking round at the cats like he didn't have a clue what was going on.

Gary my love, I said, getting the giggles. You got any pills or poppers or anything?

Yeah, I'm fucking on one here like, he shouted at me. I followed him to the ladies loo, and we locked ourselves in one of the cubicles, fumbling about. Gary always tended to sort you out for drugs, especially if you were a sumptuous beauty. He pulled out a bag of MedusaHeads and passed us one, rocking and fidgeting in the tight spot. I swallowed it down, then had to hug him because it wasn't the first time he'd saved my night.

Sure you don't want any money? I asked, kissing him on the cheek. Obviously I hadn't come up yet but it was nice to show a bit of gratitude now and then.

Naw, he said. Here get another one down you.

Then Gaz smiled really wonky like some kind of date-raper, popping another Versace on his tongue and he motioned for me to neck it off him. I was game enough – all I was interested in was that super-duper buzz, and it was never the same just doing one. I gave him a big wet snog, lifting the pill off his tongue then getting it down the hatch before he got too aroused. When we parted Gary was smiling his cheeks in half, and we waited together until the coast was clear then shot out of the cubicle. I didn't want to hang out with him the whole time, but we were laughing as we walked back to the school hall. We were gleeful going past the teachers high on E. Almost as soon as we got back in, I felt a bit of a warm feeling go up my innards and I danced to myself in the primary colours. I left Gaz gazing and leering at other girls, then went to find my own posse. Dan was around, and I pulled up next to him in my kitty-kat gear and purred, Hey there.

Alright, he smiled. All he was dressed up as was someone who wears a Moto shirt and puts gel in their hair. I wrapped my arms round his neck, and I liked it when he grabbed my hips but that's what boys always tended to do. My pills hadn't quite kicked in, but he looked gorgeous as ever and I tried to move into him. We danced for a bit, but there was nothing much to say and of all people Rachel came over and knocked around. Dan kept dancing, but he sort of lost interest and went to kiss and cuddle Rach. I could've strangled him, and I felt vulnerable on the MedusaHeads and got sad for a good five seconds. But then it was over, and I laughed when I saw Gaz bumping into people and groping one of those ugly Jealous Girls. Dancing alone, I touched the dry ice and I tried to get into the music. I grabbed my yellow bag from the dark lino since the floor was getting crowded now, and I went to boogie with Debbie on the other side. I tugged the back of her tight boob-tube up for her, then we did some funky dance moves together which we'd learnt when we were little. It was a brilliant laugh, and I decided not to tell her I'd done the ecstasy because she might get bitter. We bopped and doo-wopped, and all the dancing was getting me high as a cloud formation. My senses felt all intense and I got prickles from the music, although it was only Tina Turner and things. Taking Debbie's hand, we flashed nail varnish and headed back to our friends, and I was getting a thrill off everyone's perfumes like walking through a secret garden. Double-dropping the Es was always a bit wild – I was starting to wobble about and my mouth was getting crusty, but I felt like a princess. I smiled my cottonmouth at everybody, clinging on to Deb and trying to suppress myself from saying I loved her and how top she was. I found Dan again and grabbed the back of his speckledy white shirt, rubbing my tits up against him to some other pop thing. He slanted his head, and I nuzzled into him but all I ended up with was a half-hearted peck on the lips. I felt silly, but being on ecstasy it only lasted a moment and then I was off again. You just cannot give a fuck! I wasn't even sure why I was so desperate for Dan – he was dead good-looking, and the fact he didn't smoke was really important to me. I bow-wow-wowed my head, but I didn't let it get to me. Me and Debbie marched off to the toilet, and all we could do was get pissed and rehydrated while we crammed into one cubicle again. Our tails almost flushed down the toilet, but it felt good to be away from all the chaos. And that's when the MedusaHeads started to get ever so funny. As I stood there chewing my cheeks to pieces, a vibrant wave of something whooshed over me. The cubicle got suddenly brighter, and my hands and feet went to jelly – I was tripping like hell. At first I panicked, like the pills had been spiked with acid or something more dangerous, but I focused on the happy side and I felt not too bad. The shadows crept, and you got that 3-D effect like being in a pop-up book. My head was bobbing around at the wonder of it all, and I thought sooner or later Debbie was going to clock me being off my head.

You alright? she asked, and I laughed at the brown cat standing there. A ton of wild thoughts were going round my head, and it took loads of effort just to go, Yeah, I feel mint. I wanna find Gary.

We headed out of the cube, and god knows how we made it all the way back to the hall. It was like being in a sixties dolls' house – all these cats and puppets and people milling around, and the songs felt dead distant like they were coming from a music-box. I tried to look for Gaz – I wanted to know what was up with those Versaces. I was feeling fantastic, but it was all a bit wacky. I wandered around, breathing dead deep and seeing through the dark. I couldn't find him anywhere, and whenever someone touched me or brushed past I got slightly paranoid like they could tell I was off my box. Eventually I went to stand with the fat cat by the fire exit, which was Claire.

What's up with you? the cat said.

I'm tripping my tits off. Gaz gave us these pills, I went, getting in a daze again. On acid you really appreciated curtains and wood-finishes, and I stood around staring at everything. It was mad and dreamy, and I felt calmer being with Claire.

Yeah, he said he was having a bad one, she added. I nodded and looked at Claire's tabby-effect skirt, with the pattern slinking in and out of itself and flowing around. It was sheer pleasure. Standing there I started to feel much better, after all it wasn't every night you got a feeling like that for free. The world revolved around me, and it was très formidable.

Howay, let's dance, I said to Claire, and we went off to find the girls. The music was sounding better and better, the cymbals chinking from one ear to the other and the bass like a trampoline. I danced with my arms out, and everything up in the air was a rainbow. It reminded me of the star tent in Year Seven – the first time Dan felt my miaow. This guy came to visit us with a huge tent, and he projected all the stars onto the ceiling so you could see where Ursa Major was and where Orion's Belt was and everything. It was so romantic Dan couldn't help slipping me a finger – me and him made sure we laid down together that afternoon. This was before I was even having periods – I was shitting myself that I'd piss myself, but it actually felt alright. We only went out for about a month, and I think the star tent had something to do with the Girls becoming the Jealous Girls. Everyone fancied him in Year Seven. While I danced I could feel myself getting turned on, and I thanked the heavens I was on the trip. Who cares if the teachers knew I was on Class As – I was having a Class A time. My heart-rate was getting up and I could feel the flow of blood but it was glorious. I looked around at everybody and they were all the stars.

Adam

I got let out in time for the disco, and we arrived fashion-ably late. Abi pushed open the double doors, and we slipped through the fog of dry ice like a bunch of Russian spies. None of us bothered putting on fancy dress – we wanted to be cool, but all we saw when we got inside were kittens, pirates and vampires. There were a lot of people dancing, but all we did was stand in the corner and try not to be embarrassing. Me and Burny tried to get pissed round his beforehand, slugging half of his mum's Martini with our heads in the cupboard. I had a bit of tunnel vision from it, and I knew I was getting tipsy because I kept looking Abi up and down and I didn't even fancy her. Donna was look-ing super too, but I decided to stop perving before I got a bit of a lob-on. Now and then Abi tried to talk to me with our backs to the wall, but the music was too blaring and I wasn't making much sense. I had no idea the sorts of things you had to talk to girls about. Shoes? Make-up? I kept an eye out for Eve or anyone, but the hall was full of boys chasing girls and I doubted I'd make a massive impact.

'Some fucking mint birds in here like,' the Prick said, and I shrugged but I knew what he meant. He wouldn't get any action though, and neither would I – it wasn't prom night full of LA Sun Valley virgins, it was Brackenhoe Christmas disco. There was even a bit of dogshit on the floorboards someone had tramped in – how disgusting. I felt a bit like crap and all.

'I love your shirt,' Abi said in the Prick's ear, but it was only his Blockbuster outfit with the name-tag pulled off. Me and Burny pissed off the Prick because we got pissed without him, but we were just that much cooler than him. Abi always had to flirt with someone though – I figured it was all that exotic Latin blood in her. She was quite dark, and whenever you went to her house you felt like you were in an Aztec temple or a Jennifer Lopez video.

'Do you want to dance?' she went on, but that Prick completely screwed his face up and yelled at her, 'No; I'm not a dickhead.'

I laughed, then my heart popped. Finally I spotted Eve and her mates – they looked like sex goddesses in the cat clothes, but they were bopping around with a bunch of lads and Eve was clinging on to Dan Williams, and the jealousy hit like a thunderbolt. The Martini wasn't really doing its stuff – she was a black cat and she walked across my path. I twiddled my thumbs. I'd probably be hungover by ten o'clock, and I probably wouldn't even speak to anyone and probably go home feeling upset. I wanted to get myself amongst the girls, but whenever I shook my hips Abi and Donna giggled because a shy kid getting jiggy looks so out of place. I was straight out of a Smiths song.

'You want to dance with me?' Abi asked, probably out of sympathy. I pretended to mull it over in case she was taking the piss, but she dragged me out anyway. I hadn't really danced before except in front of the mirror, but I shook myself about as we careened towards Rachel and her friends, out the way of the dog crap of course. I tried to touch Abi's hips, but she turned her head away and it felt like dancing with a dead girl. I liked the feel of the white corset thing she had on, but I hated girls thinking boys only ever had one thing on their minds. I was just trying to be friendly, but it was the fuck-off-don't-kiss-me face.

'That's enough,' Abi said, then she hugged her cousin Rachel and chatted with her instead of hanging around with me. She pulled her fingers through her dark hair, laughing about the cat outfits and the whiskers. I turned 180 degrees and tried to smile at her, but Rach frowned and mouthed, 'Who's that?'

My cheeks burned red disco lights. All of a sudden I had no one to dance with, spotlit on an empty stage, and I froze up. I was only trying to be light and floaty and outgoing, but when it comes down to it you'll always be the same boring bastard. Were you supposed to just go and grab whoever you wanted? I danced and glanced at Eve but her eyes were shut and she was in a world of her own. I thought fuck it. I scrunched my gel then shuffled into the middle of the floor, doing the seed-sowing dance with my arms jerking out at the sides. My hands looked a bit creepy in the lights, and I felt like a sex pest. It was getting near to half-nine, and the dancefloor was so crowded I kept losing sight of Eve. Occasionally I caught a glimpse of a swishing blonde pony-tail, but apart from that she was a bit of a mystery. I squinted around, then felt Dan Williams grab me and shout, 'You're going for it tonight, aren't you! Come dance with us; you're a mint laugh.'

I wasn't sure if he was taking the piss or not; he was mates with Burny, but we never really talked and I didn't want to dance around for his amusement. But his face was pretty sincere so I smiled and slipped into a gap. I looked about the circle of Rachel, Gracie, Jenni Farrell, Gaz, Claire Blame, Debbie and Eve. It was dreamy – I stamped quickly to the music then grinned at Debbie when she waved. She always seemed dead caring and genuine, not bitchy or up herself, but she had a boyfriend. She looked surprised to see me waving my arms about like an electric-shock victim, and for the hilarity of it she pulled me over for a little one-on-one. I hopped over the handbags as our soft hands tugged, and I felt my elbow glide off Gracie's big boobs and I was getting all excitable. My heart was skipping to the beat of a brilliant night, and I did not want to fuck it up. Like a pervert with Tourette's I was trying to harness all thoughts of sex and wanks and explosions, but the testosterone was fluttering out of me like a gymnast with the ribbon. Debbie's skin felt warm and smooth and she was dancing quite intimate with me, but after a minute or so I decided to let go because I didn't want that fuck-off face again. I felt deranged enough to swap her gently for Eve. At first she flinched but she didn't pull away – I was a happy puppy, running after cats and pink toilet-roll. Eve laughed – her face looked both shocked and very smiley. We did a silly erotic dance together, and she gave me a big kiss on the cheek leaving two wet cherry lips. She was delumptious. And from then on all I wanted to do was get home and wet myself into a million pink toilet-rolls. I was desperate for her, but I spent the rest of the night on the other side of the circle, making sure no one tried to flirt with her during some boy-band ballads. Once or twice we caught each others' eye and smiled. It was a complete dream. At the end of the night I spun round to find Burny and everyone, all knackered and ready to go, and I caught up with Eve before she slinked into the night.

'Hiya,' I said, smiling sweetly in the dark. 'Did you have a good night?'

'Yeah,' she pouted, flicking her fringe round as she joined me in the queue. 'I'm shattered though.'

'Me too – I've been sowing so many seeds tonight, I might as . . .'

I couldn't even think up a punchline, but Eve laughed pretty loud as we made it out in the cold. She pretended to hit me in the biceps, and as we looked out across the car park it felt like we were an item. She was wobbling about and I thought about touching her. Gary Clinton barged past as people knocked around, aching my left shoulder but I didn't care. I kissed Eve night-night then joined my friends by the litter bins. I got a few looks of spite and jealousy – Abi for one didn't like Eve – but gorgeous girls were always bitching about each other and nothing was going to bring me down. I held my head against the breeze and watched all the cars going nowhere. I wouldn't get to sleep that night.

Gary

We ground down a couple of the pills and snorted them. The bus was rocking so we left them dead gritty, and when we got to the disco our noses were in fuckin ribbons. I kept swallowing loads of blood as we watched out the window. There was grief in Park End – I'd been over Ste's for another hundred MedusaHeads, and while we sat in his bedroom listening to the Beltram tape he was telling me all his fuckin shite.

'Yeah so little Caroline's been fucked about by Watson out of our year you know,' he went as we laid about counting out the pills. Caroline was Ste's sister and I'd definitely had a few wanks over her like, but Watson had been fucking her since she started secondary school, then fucking some other cow in Berwick Hills, then coming back to Park End and giving Caroline some hepatitis or whatever it was. It was all Ste could talk about. I didn't know what hepatitis was, but after I shagged Gemma Rover in September I got some stinking scab on my dick-shaft and it was probably worse than that. Nowadays I went for cleaner, cannier girls – with Claire Blame under my belt and a handjob off Debbie Forrester, I could nail whoever I wanted. I figured all them lasses would be at the disco, and with the pills kicking in I started to lighten up. But it felt more like we'd done acid tabs because the bus seats were starting to turn to rock-hard porcelain, and I wasn't on a proper happy buzz. I blamed it on Ste. About once a month we got together a hundred pound for a hundred of his cousin's ecstasies, but it was the first time we'd seen Versaces and once you start necking them you can't really take them back. Ste's cousin was pretty reliable for pills and that, but he was an ugly cunt and when we went round that afternoon he was saying he was off the pills for good and it made you wonder. He'd keep cutting us a deal for money's sake, but if you're not mixing business with pleasure there's something up. We carved our names into the bus seats then got off at the Beechwood Easterside, my head going about a million miles an hour. A massive stream of girls and policemen and STDs was rushing about in there like a red hot tap. They were weird gurns. We necked one more though for the buzz, and as we sloped across the field I was certain the grass was like five or six times longer.

The school hall was sinister when we got inside. Everyone was dressed different and all me and Ste wanted to do was stand in the corner with some mates, decked out in trackie bees. He was depressing the fuck out of me, like he'd only come out to look for Watson and get him brayed. Watson was pretty well connected with these lads from Grove Hill, but me and Ste knew hard cunts all over town and in the end Watson didn't even show. Even so Ste had a long face all night, and I couldn't be arsed wasting my time with him. I walked alone following the pattern on the floorboards, feeling pissed off and I couldn't see anyone I wanted to talk to. I stood for a while round the catgirls, and it was only when Claire Blame nudged me that I realised it was those lot. She grinned a circus mouth and asked how I was, but my eyes were all over the shop and I told her I was having a bad one. I was in a fuckin state like. I fell in the direction of Eve, and when she asked me for pills I got paranoid what with fifty of the cunts in my back pocket. All the teachers were standing round the walls like PCs. I sorted Eve out in the bogs though, away from all the shite back there, and I wasn't bothered about money cos I wanted to offload the MedusaHeads as soon as I could. To be honest I was thinking about flushing them down the fuckin bog, but

I'd have to twoc a load more sportswear to afford another hundred and I wasn't that arsed. After Eve snogged me for another pill I started getting all horny and thinking I wanted to fuck her head off, but I had to get out of that cubicle. In there I was seeing all sorts of twisting walls and breathing doors. It was fuckin acid or ket alright, but I didn't say owt. We walked together back to the hall, chasing Eve's tail at about one mile an hour. I took in a huge breath, had a shiver and I felt dead tall compared to the furniture. The curtains kept opening and shutting in time with the music, and the dancefloor was revolving. It was suddenly fuckin beauty, and I was totally off my box. I floated along with the girls, and all I wanted to do was stick my dick in between their whiskers. Debbie had nip-ons through her boob-tube, and Eve left not much to the imagination if you get me. But for the rest of the night I couldn't touch her. This moron from Jason Burn's form had found his way into our group, and though no one knew him all of a sudden he was dancing with the best girls. He was dancing like a cunt mind. Debbie and Eve grabbed him and spun him round, and as I watched the room got darker and melted – I felt all paralysed. On LSD you think you've got everyone sussed out, but I watched him dart around like a fuckin homo and yet still there was something going on between him and Eve. Everything in my head started to centre around them two, like that cunt had been put on earth to ruin my night. And I got myself in a bit of a hole, all these sick thoughts charging round in a vicious circle and I ground my teeth down to little stumps. My skull was fuckin banging and I had to go sit with Ste after all, and I couldn't say anything.

At the end of the disco me and Ste were baltic in the rain

in the car park, waiting with Claire Blame for the minibus she ordered. She was shivering in her cat gear, and we shared a bit of Smirnoff Ice she'd taxed while everyone piled out of the wall. I was still tripping out, and while I smoked one of Ste's Regals I was watching the smoke twist into bikes and trains and motor vehicles. I must've been desperate to get home, after all it was a fuckin shit night. There was no chance of getting laid, especially since Claire had a bun in the oven, and I waited for Eve and that cunt to walk out together laughing at some shite thing he said. They kissed goodnight and I wanted to fuckin batter him. His face was a monkey mask, and he hunched towards his friends like a cunt that got the cream. The school and the cars were wobbling, and as I glared across at that lad he had the nerve to wink at me like we were all matey. He thought he was Mr Popular. And then my whole night was fixed around snapping him in half.

'Fuckin fight you now then, daft cunt,' I shouted over. The park became a videogame, and as I walked I dropped the Ice bottle and throttled the fuck out of him. You could make out certain voices laughing around us, and even though I'd lost all perspective I landed a couple of decent punches. His head and my hand met somewhere in the middle of space, and I grunted as a few chunks of tooth flew out his mouth and the jaw snapped. As he fell to the ground, I kept hold of his collar and booted the cunt full in the face, the Nike shooting high up as his nose buckled in. He curled up in a bit of blood, and I stopped for a sec looking at how red it was. Everything was quite stop–start on the acid, and I had to proper focus when I reached over for the bottle. It was already broken after dropping it ten feet and I mashed the pointed edge right into his eye, severing the lid and hopefully a bit of ball and all. I had dogshit on my trainers as well from walking through the twenty-inch grass, but Jason Burn grappled me and told me to fuck off. He was fairly sound; I shrugged him off and I felt like the lights were switched on again in my head. His mate was a red stain, but at least he wouldn't go anywhere near Eve again. I clocked that Abi Ellis crying slightly behind me – she was another lass I wouldn't kick out of bed, even though she had a load of tarbrush in her. I turned and headed back to the minibus – I still felt everyone's eyes on me but it could've been the paranoia and that. You could see Donna Easter sticking a red tissue to the daft little shit's face, and when I got back to Claire all she could say was, 'Look what you've done, you dick.'

But what did she know. As we stumbled onto the minibus, we sat towards the back and I rubbed my right hand – I'd swollen it from hitting him too hard, but mebbies my mind was exaggerating it. We didn't talk much as the bus rushed down the street, but I think Claire was tired. I was still tripping slightly and I brought my knees up to my chest and I needed to get some kip. When I woke up I wasn't totally sure what had gone on.

Chapter Eleven

Boxing Day

Adam

I spent the holiday in ward 9. I couldn't eat any Christmas food til I came back from the dentist, and even then it didn't taste good and I cried through the telly. For a bit my mouth was like a grand piano smashed, and once the front ones got capped it looked like a shitty tatty keyboard out of Music. I sat with my face in the curtains, getting lower and lower the more I thought about stuff. I pressed the neat blue stitches on my nose, then winced and wrapped myself in the bed sheets. I couldn't sleep at all. The left eye-lid was hanging off with the white bit all red and tender, and my jaw felt twice as big as I sat and watched the sun curve round the hospital. It was boring but I didn't notice the days flying by – Christmas Day was the same as a Monday morning. Mum and Dad came now and then, and for Christmas they got me the fake Telecaster I'd seen in Cash Converters but it was at home and all they brought to the hospital for me was crackers and that. The jokes and the mottos were agonising.

'Look what happens when you go picking fights,' Dad said to me on the first day, but he really didn't get it. I was too pained to explain. 'You're not as tough as you think.'

Well I was finding that out alright. I cried my eyes out at

the dentist, the nerves all exposed like electric wire and them going mad carving my mouth out. It was sheer horror. I had to wait a couple of weeks to get the caps made, and until then I wasn't eating any solids – the last day at the dentist was the last day shitting out water. Then there was a day or two of horrifying eye surgery, afterwards wearing a daft eye-patch like the saddest pirate on the seven seas.

When I got home I plugged the guitar in, but I wasn't having any luck learning from the Beatles book – none of the happy songs made much sense to me anyway. Messing about with the amp you could get the fuzzy sound of 'Revolution' or 'She Said She Said', but god knows what the notes were – I knew what it felt like to be dead though. 'Yer Blues' was in constant rotation on the turntable, and I was certainly in my blue period.

I thought the Christmas disco had gone okay until Gary punched my lights out. Did I really dance with Eve? I'd been slurping so much anaesthetic I couldn't remember any more what were dreams. At hospital all the nurses seemed more like skeletons in miniskirts than Benny Hill characters, and my interest in girls was dwindling. I wasn't going to get close to any nice ladies with a face like a building site anyhow. All there was to do was sit around moping – it was actually a blessing that I didn't have the guitar, since I was so shit at it and I didn't want all the kids on the ward thinking I was a div. Ever since I got into the Beatles it was my dream to get good on an instrument, travel round the world, break loads of hearts, but all I could do was break my jaw on Brackenhoe car park. In hospital the obsessive-compulsiveness got worse – I went round shutting toilet doors and ward curtains millions of times. I was a nervy wreck. No one came to visit me at James Cook, except for Abi on Boxing Day and she brought with her a bunch of grapes. She'd been pretty caring since the accident, always phoning and gobbing on about Easterside and everything going on, and she kept my mind off things. She hadn't seen Gaz since the disco, nor had she seen Burny or the Prick or anyone else for that matter. I hardly even saw a text off them.

'So how you feeling anyways?' Abi asked as she sat on the plastic grey chair. Since I'd been knocked out she tended to put on this cute annoying voice, and me being the paranoid type I always thought she was talking down to me. But she had such a mouth on her you never really had to say that much to her.

'Okay, you know, not too bad,' I replied, watching the silver winter light blast over her. 'Have a good Christmas?'

'Oh yeah, not bad. You'll never guess what happened though . . . you know Linda, my cousin? Not on the Shannon side; the other side. Yeah well her and her boyfriend just got engaged. It's mad, they've only known each other five minutes and that. We were thinking she's got pregnant, you know, but like she's a fat cow anyway so you'd never notice. So what did you get off Santa?'

'Oh this and that. Money really,' I said. I couldn't be bothered bringing up the guitar or the amp getting all fuzzy-wuzzy – she'd only want to come round and have a listen.

'Class, well we'll have to go out again sometime soon. You can treat us,' she laughed, but it wasn't all that hilarious. I hadn't really thought about going out ever again – after the mad disco violence it didn't really seem like I was cut out for it. But Abi's face was a floodlight, and she went, 'We'll get out of Easterside though. Town's miles better – there's always knobheads, but we'll keep you out of trouble . . .'

I didn't like Abi taking the mick, however Eve was always mouthing off about town with her mates and I really wanted to bump into her again. I was totally hung up about her – I imagine Gaz gave me a hiding because I was twirling about with her and being daft on the dancefloor, but when you're laid in hospital with your face dropping off it's not like things can get much worse. Eve was lovely. And now Abi was looking out for me, not that I needed a spic barbie-doll for a bodyguard. But she had been really good to me, and even if she was always talking down to me I would've gone mentally ill if she wasn't around. We sat and chewed the grapes, her picking off the skins between her gnashers and looking about the place.

'So when do you get out of here, then?' she asked. The hospital was depressing as fuck, all mouldy green and white with metal and sad faces darting about the place, but Abi was my lucky mascot.

'I dunno, a couple of days I suppose. I'll be out in time for school, anyway.'

'Aw, good. Bless you, chuck.'

I swallowed more grapes and I felt happyish. My parents wouldn't be keen on letting me out the house again, but I was starting not to give a shit about them. If I wasn't getting beaten up outdoors I was only getting beaten up indoors, and I had to make my own mistakes not stay wrapped in cotton wool all my life. Plus they'd started my pocket money again, probably out of sympathy for being a total failure, so it wasn't all bad.

Me and Abi polished off the grapes, and she didn't know how brilliant she was, taking me under her wing. I peeled back the covers, and I risked smiling even though it split my lips up. All of a sudden I didn't have any stitches or cracked bones or dog muck for blood. The bed felt comfy and the mattress relaxed. Viva the señorita.

Eve

Get another one down your neck, Jenni said. She'd brought in loads of her sweeties from Christmas, and we sat scoffing them with the boys that breaktime. There was always that dull feeling being back at school after a good holiday, but it was great to see everyone again. Mam got me and my sisters a haircut at Toni+Guy for Christmas, and I came to school that day with gold blonde layers and super sculpting. I was straddling Matty Tyler and the bench, and I looked good. I wasn't upset about Gary getting excluded – you hardly noticed as we all crowded in the circle shape. I took another piece of Dairy Milk and licked the heck out of it. I got laid a couple of times over Crimbo – me and Matty got busy on New Year's Eve, but there's always that slightly nervous feeling when you start doing it with someone new. I wasn't sure if the butterflies were because I wanted to be with him, or because I didn't want to be with him. I liked Rachel's style – she still reckoned she wanted to be single, although she was quite wrapped up in Dan as we laid about the bench. Ever since the disco they'd been knocking around together loads, but the other night on the phone she said they were just mates. Perhaps they were just squeaking the bed. I played with my sharp fringe, wriggling on Matty's knee – he was a great lad, but I wasn't sure if I wanted the whole ordeal of dating and spending money and riding to Pallister Park every few days. All of that just for a boring

Missionary. I told Debbie he was pretty uncreative in bed – I always liked him from English because he was the first lad to get stubble, but I figured I'd stop phoning him and get out of the relationship as quick as poss. It was hardly even a relationship – we wouldn't talk much at school, and when he was round Matty only tended to say a few words before we got snogging and end up between the sheets. I wasn't even paying much attention to him as the girls chattered round the circle.

So when's your mam and dad leaving again? Jenni went, looking Rachel's way. Jenni was trying to lose weight for the new year – that's why we had so many sweets that breaktime. She wasn't really that chubby – I thought she'd be better off fixing those wonky boobs, personally. But we stuffed our faces no matter what.

Dunno, about a month or two. Just before we go to Majorca, Rach replied, sucking and licking her way through a caramel finger and I laughed, thinking of Dan's tail. For some reason me and Rachel could put anything in our mouths and not put on any weight.

But you're defo having a party, though? I asked, raising an eyebrow. Rachel nodded, and I watched her stroke Danny's arm under the white shirt sleeve. I was happy for them. Rachel's parents were going to Antigua for a fortnight in March, and it was always a good laugh taking a load of drink and whatnot into someone's house and being wallys. The last time we'd done that was round Fairhurst's though, back when he touched Rachel's tit and got dumped. Boys were dafties.

God, have you seen Adam! Matty said over my shoulder. The bell had gone for next lesson, and little Adam from Art came sauntering past with a huge red blotch where a fist had been. I hadn't thought of him much since the disco, but I remember feeling awful when Gaz knocked him out. That night the MedusaHeads were insane, and as it was pills tended to blotch your memory up. A few people like Matty and Ste Barber and Jenni pointed and laughed, but I nearly welled up – us lot were sort of born on shooting stars and we didn't even know it. Kids like Adam always tended to walk around with a sad face, like they hated the world and wanted to murder everyone. He wasn't even that bad looks-wise, just a bit strange round the edges. I guessed I wouldn't be seeing Matty again after all – as we walked separate ways to French and History, I realised he was shitty as everybody else. I liked Adam – we had a good time together on disco night. And lads were cunts – for example Claire Blame was huge now, there was only a couple of months left til the baby flew out and there was still no daddy. You can't let boys take control of your life, but all the same you've got to have one. I almost chased after Adam as the corridor filled up, to say sorry about everything and for a few of us laughing. But he'd probably think I was taking the mick, and want to murder me.

Chapter Twelve

Daddy's Girl

Eve

I learnt a new word in French that day: l'hôpital. I'd hardly set foot in a hospital for ages, then all of a sudden Mam was getting chemotherapy and Claire was getting her baby pulled out. We went to visit them quite often – Claire wanted us to be there as soon as her waters broke. It was disgusting. Me and Jenni got a lift with Natasha, and you couldn't look past the curtain when she was squeezing out the kid. I held Claire's sweaty palm as she groaned and moaned – me and Jenni didn't want to see her miaow all big and stretchy, and it totally put you off getting pregnant. The Baby Boy was beautiful though, and we helped Claire out with some homework while the baby hung in incubation. It was pretty obvious she'd be quitting school anyhow. Every three weeks we went with Mam for the chemo stuff – she said she didn't want us nicking off lessons just to see her, but to be honest it was taking its toll on me going backwards and forwards to Brackenhoe to home to James Cook and back again. I was a dead girl walking. That evening I'd hardly stepped through the door when Laura and Natasha dragged me into the red Vauxhall, and we charged back towards Marton Road. Mam looked really gaunt in one of those greeny-white nighties, and her hair was fallen out and she was huffing and puffing. She reckoned she still felt the tumour, but I guessed the doctors knew what they were doing. They reckoned the chemotherapy was going quite positive. I didn't cry when I saw her, but we were all shivery round the bed while she spluttered. We spent ages at l'hôpital feeling edgy. Some nights Mam was chirpy and some nights she was knackered – the night Claire went home with the baby was the night Mam could hardly speak, throwing up all the time and looking awful. Me and my sisters crept round the bed, watching her lay about like a shipwreck – eventually we had to leave her to it, and we walked back to the car park in complete silence. It was starting to dawn on us Mam might not live for ever. But we managed to look on the bright side, and Natasha drove us to KFC for a bucket full of spicy wings – we sucked it off our fingers while we shot towards South Bank. In a corny way Mam's cancer made us think about our dad and what he was up to, and it really made you realise how precious your life is. I gazed out the window all the way there – Natasha was driving through the fog with her full-beams on, and it was the look of heaven outside. We liked the idea of surprising our dad, and he'd also want to know how Mam was doing. He wasn't all cold-hearted although he was lazy (he wanted to collect the dole while Mam grafted at the Spacker School), and you've got to love your daddy. His new girlfriend had the look of Jo Guest but not half as sexy, and I think they copped off too soon after the divorce, though I wasn't the suspicious type and I didn't care what he did with his life. He had a Joint Claim now with the new bird.

Do you think Dad'll borrow me some money? I asked

from the back of the Vauxhall. I crossed my legs in those tight school trousers, watching white chemical factories whizz past the window. I could hardly tell what was smoke and what was mist.

For what? Natasha asked. She was ever so bossy now Mam was out of action and now she was married.

Friday night, I said simply. I think Rach and Debbie and everyone's going to Empire or somewhere.

Natasha just shrugged and sighed, and I breathed breath on the glass. Laura shivered in her furry coat, just as we reached South Bank and the sign that said FROM HOPE TO REALITY. I didn't get it – South Bank was still pretty scruffy. All the terraces looked like they were lined with sharks' teeth, the jagged glass being there to keep out intruders and other unsavouries. We used to feel grown-up letting ourselves into our dad's new pad at weekends – he always made pizza and chips for us and sometimes took us down Redcar for a play on the beach or a cassette out of Woolworth's. We used to write our names big in the sand, stamping out the letters on tippy-toes. Such fun.

The industry smell must've reminded her; Natasha pulled up on Costa Street then suddenly went, Shit, I'd better get petrol actually.

Can I let myself in first? I went, leaning into the gap between sisters. Natasha nodded, then sped off into the night as I hopped onto the concrete. Costa Street was nasty – a lot of the houses were boarded up like in Beechwood, but at least we had a view over the playing field not an orangey scrapyard. Saying that, there were a few kids out playing and the streetglow was glinting on the rusty metal and I smiled to myself. The fog was clearing. I tried to quietly unlock Dad's door – it'd been ages since he'd seen us and I liked that element of surprise. Even though I didn't like her Liz was quite canny – she always forced us tea and stuff, but we were the classic step-daughters and just grunted through any conversation. I stepped out of my school shoes in the hallway then snuck along in green SEXY BABE socks, following the sound of the telly. Spotting a twenty-pound note on the shelf, I smiled thinking Dad must be loaded although there was also a box of Benson and I thought he might've stopped smoking after Mam and everything. I curled my face and rehearsed what I'd say to him. I held my breath and I jumped, but I jumped into an empty living room. The television was talking to itself – often you had to do that to ward off burglars, but Dad hardly went out on weekdays and in any case I could hear a bit of mumbling upstairs. I wasn't fussed about watching *EastEnders* so I snuck out the lounge again, going upstairs like a kitty on the prowl. That reminded me of the Medusa night – we still had to return those cat ears and tails, all stained with drink and kisses. At the top of the stairs the noises stopped. Their bedroom door was a bit ajar and I started pushing it open until I spotted them in the mirror shagging each other on the double bed. Liz was on top and her white tits shook while my dad tried to keep going underneath. He was blowing out air like a factory, his hairy legs dead tensed under Liz's bum. It was the first time I'd seen them naked, and I didn't stand there that long. Yuck! Feeling dizzy, I pushed my eyes shut then sneaked downstairs, absolutely plagued. I felt ill perching on the bottom step, as if my dad was cheating on Mam while she was having her body zapped, except he wasn't. I put my knees together while I sat there, wondering if I could really ask Dad and Liz for money now I'd seen them fucking. I decided to forget it. But I only had brown pennies in my Halifax account, and there was no chance of babysitting little Nicole really or doing any jobs for Mam. Then suddenly I remembered Dad's twenty on the hall shelf and I just could not resist it. What a naughty girl. I guessed it was better to be greedy than sad, so I reached and slipped the money in my Duffer pocket, then stepped into the foggy light and waited on the kerb for Laura and Natasha. I tried to be silent as I could. The whole of Teesside was humming brown, black and tangerine and I looked through the mist for the outline of roofs and power stations. Sooner or later it got boring on your own – while I sat a couple of kids pretended to ride over my toes on their BMXs, which was just charming. I touched the twenty in my jacket then popped my cheeks out as Natasha pulled up again in the Vauxhall.

Isn't he in? she asked, jumping out. She walked round checking all the car doors were locked, but I couldn't imagine anyone wanting to steal that piece of rubbish. It was nothing like Fairhurst's Citroën with the alloys and the big exhaust and the dump valves and all that other stuff that goes whoosh and zoom. The word dump used to make me laugh though. I lifted myself from the kerb then straightened my trousers and said, Yeah, he's upstairs. He's shagging Liz!

I said it with a bit of a smile. All Laura could do was raise her eyebrow, and she went, You're full of shit.

I just shrugged it off like a cool dude. Shaking her head, Natasha clopped her Nike trainers over the pavement then knocked hard on the cardboard door. We had his keys, but I think Natasha was scared of his hairy legs after all. We stood running our fingers through our hair while we waited, and Natasha laughed out of her nose when Dad appeared in just his bathrobe. It was dead obvious. He lifted his curly eyebrows then smiled, recognising us in the fog, but he didn't look that flustered. I could well imagine Liz spread-eagled upstairs, keeping the bed warm.

Hi girls – I wasn't expecting to see youse round here, Dad said, letting us in.

Well no, Natasha mumbled, and inside we all burst out laughing but kept a straight face. I kicked off my shoesies again and went back into the living room. Dad ran upstairs to finish something while we made ourselves comfy, and I tried to keep my mind on *EastEnders* instead of the twenty. We squashed up on the patterned sofa, tapping each other and giggling. I put the tips of blonde fringe in my mouth, then felt my stomach turn over even though we'd gone for the KFC.

You hungry or something, Laura laughed, so I took it out. We all had our new haircuts. When Dad and Liz finally came into the lounge, they were wearing their casuals but I couldn't help still imagining them naked. Knowing it was wrong only made me think about it more.

Eve, didn't you want to ask Dad something? Natasha went, nudging me and I felt my cheeks blow up. At first I thought she meant the sex, then I remembered the money and said softly, Oh. Naw. It doesn't matter now.

Natasha lifted the sides of her mouth – she thought I wasn't a selfish cow any more, but actually I was a bit worse than that. All I wanted was to go out on Friday night but, as

I crossed my legs on the scratchy sofa, I wondered if I'd cursed it. I felt a bit weird around my dad, but not because of the sex – in fact I thought it was pretty cool him and Liz had a good shag life. I hoped I would at that age. I sat there and curled the note in my fingers, and I said to myself I'd find a nice bloke and I'd have good sex with him too. And I'd never steal again.

Chapter Thirteen

Black Lungs One

Adam

Abi took me out on Friday. I had to let my hair down, but in fact I gelled it up with the Brylcreem and threw on the new shirt I bought over the Christmas period. That number I wore at the disco got all caked in blood, but instead of sticking it in the washing-machine I chucked it over next-door's fence and went on my own to Marks and Sparks when I got out of hospital. Funnily enough the shirt I pipped for was maroon, so I wouldn't make the same mistake again. I didn't like spending money and I was totally clueless when it came to fashion – I considered asking Abi to take me round those trendy boutiques down Linthorpe Road, but they were way too expensive and in any case I wasn't hip enough for those extravagant garments. My face was still a bit contorted from all the beatings, and I could bend my nose now like it was a rubber dildo.

Everything I did over that time was wrapped in woolly sadness. I was sort of sulking in the back of the taxi with Abigail, but she kept touching my leg and chattering away and I didn't mean to be annoying. She was being nice to me. The Paki in the front kept looking at us as Abi talked and talked, and I still enjoyed her gossip even though I'd heard most of it two or three times already. Now and then when she wasn't looking the driver stared down her blouse. She was telling me about Claire Blame getting pregnant, Rachel her cousin shagging Dan Williams after the disco, and how there were tons of boys at school on drugs and stuff. I felt so boring – for example the Beatles had done all sorts of narcotics and even they were quite clean-cut at the beginning of the sixties. My wildest moment was probably getting Eve to dance with me and then not doing anything.

It was about eight or eight thirty when we got to the Royal Exchange, and we chipped in a few pound for the pervert Paki then walked in separately. It was nerve-wracking with all the bouncers staring you up and down, and I feared getting turned away or even receiving another hiding. I'd become a complete fanny, but Abi looked after me. We squashed past tracksuits and shirts to some seats near the back, drinking lagers and Smirnoffs and screaming in each other's ears. Now and then I tried to say something funny but she never quite caught it. Loads of lads in there were pumped up on steroids – you could tell by the square shoulders and blockheads and tiny cocks. I avoided eye-contact. I wondered why people would want to come out to kick each other's heads in, rather than having a good time. But I guessed it was the same as me coming out all depressed and nervous – some people are nutcases.

'So you reckon your Rachel and them might be out tonight?' I yelled at Abi, and she nodded. I was more interested in Eve – just laying eyes on her was like reaching enlightenment, or at least it made me wee my pants. But I guessed she only went out with musclebound pricks, the type that give you protection but also chlamydia and other odd things. I glanced about the bar again, and all round us the boys looked like they wanted to throttle each other. I watched *Raging Bull* in the Christmas holiday, and I practised punching the wall and lifting my bed-frame but I only knacked myself. I tried to build myself up by stuffing my face and using the skipping-rope, but if anyone saw me I might as well have been a little girl in a daisy garden. One afternoon I was getting frustrated in the bathroom, throwing punches at the silly cunt in the mirror, and I ended up putting my hand through it. Blood ran down my knuckles like strawberry sauce on a sundae, and I went back into my bedroom with seven years' bad luck.

'You alright, honey?' Abi asked, rubbing my thigh. It caught me off guard and a bit of Carling went down the wrong way; I tried not to splutter it all over her. I gasped and smiled. I was a stupid idiot. Abi was giving me all these strange come-hither signals, but she had loads of admirers at school and there was no reason for her making a move on me. I had mashed potato for a head. To be honest I thought she was taking the piss out of me and I found her faintly irritating.

Abi kind of screwed her face up, then flipped a Regal out of her bag and sucked on that instead. I watched her blow the sky out of her mouth. Ever since the disco incident I had a shopping list of things to do to get macho, for instance drinking, smoking, muscles, haircut, clothes, swearing, pumping. It's weird sometimes having to be fake just to get what you want, but everyone's doing it. I never really wanted to smoke in my life, but I had to start somewhere and I went to Abi, 'Can I get a bit of that?'

I nodded at the Regal, and she crunched her forehead then passed it over. I headrushed. Burny used to slag off kids on the playground never taking any of the smoke back, but I was swallowing it all down my gullet and it was sickening. On programmes like *Saved by the Bell* or *Neighbours* it's always the geeks who cough out the first puff – I resisted the temptation but my throat was spasming and I was obviously screwing my face up. I sat there and smoked away without inhaling at all. I felt the big man.

And just then Eve and the girls wandered in. I got a twisty feeling in my tummy, looking at them all dressed to kill and not knowing what to do with myself. I just sat and tried to hold the Regal in a charismatic way. I wondered if I should keep glancing or play hard to get or muscle my way over, but in the end it was Abi who did the honours. Abi held my hand as we swept over to the bar – I wanted to look like I was going out with her and not at the same time. Luckily I dragged my pint with us so I had something to do while Abi hugged Rachel and chatted and pretended I didn't exist. I kept playing with the cuffs of the maroon shirt and I hated myself for it. I couldn't keep still. After a bit I realised Eve was catching my eye, and as she came over I got in a whirl of nerves and emotion and the neon lights began twirling.

'Is that a ladder in your tights or a stairway to heaven / Did it hurt when you fell from heaven / Get your coat love you've pulled,' is what I could've said, but instead there was silence and I went, 'Er hello.'

'Hey, how you doing?' she asked, her eyes hovering a little on my scabs. By accident my hand went up there, but that was pretty scabby too after the incident with the mirror. At least the eye-patch was gone – I'd stayed at home while I was getting healed, but even odd jaunts to

Easterside Bells resulted in Pretty Polly and peg-leg jokes.

'Not too bad. You having a good night?' I asked, shifting from foot to foot. At home in your dreams it seems so easy to come across as a Cary Grant type full of one-liners, but in reality I could hardly speak to anyone without quaking or trying to hide behind the sofa.

'Yeah, it's okay. Who you out with?' Eve asked, and I pointed at Abigail Ellis. 'Are youse an item then?'

'Naw,' I said. Eve was absolutely stunning; she was born with Barbie bones and Sindy curves, whereas I felt more like a plastic dog-crap. For all I knew some hard-case was about to come and knock my block off again. And I carried on flinching and twitching.

'You're not still bothered about Gaz, are you?' she went. I wondered if it was that obvious I was a mental patient. She grabbed the side of my face so I could hear in all the noise, and went to me, 'Don't worry about him. He's a dick.'

The words were angels' trumpets. I touched her hip, and suddenly everything felt good. In fact it was like the black cloud above my head had toddled off. Girls' hands were all over me, and I was growing up. Oh god and I was smoking as well – I reached over to Abi and plucked another ciga-rette from her hand, making sure to blow it all round me and Eve. I wrapped us up in a little white blanket. She looked all surprised, and she also looked blurry when she asked me, 'How long you been smoking, you bad boy?'

I pulled the cherub face, then lied, 'Aw about six month. On and off, you know.'

It was the sort of thing you'd hear Burny saying. After that night I wasn't even sure I wanted to smoke at all, it happened to be smelly and clench your lungs up and get your fingers yellow. But the point of it was looking cool and being naughty and at least I'd done that. I smoked about five more that night, putting them out well before the sickly end and not even taking them back. The only feeling I got was feeling ever so dirty in the morning.

Eve

Sparkly two-inch heels, sky-bluey dress, glitter bag, gold necklace, bangle earrings, the Urban Decay eyeshadow and ruby glaze lips, Natasha's mascara black or was it brown, blue eyeliner out of Avon, wax legs, a couple of gold rings and French Connection watch, Burberry Brit, high pony-tail, white Calvin Klein underwear, and my dad's twenty pound. All of that as I staggered down Beechwood Avenue.

We purchased more ecstasy on Friday night, and we continued to get off our heads. I suppose if you were to die tomorrow you'd hope you made the most of your life on earth, but it was hard thinking about that with Mam so ill. Me and my sisters chipped in for a Chinese from Marton shops, and we crunched prawn crackers round the telly taking care of her. She was home again and pretty delicate, and she had hard breathing but you got used to that after a while and gossip-wise she was her usual self. Mam told us all the nurses' names and who they were sleeping with. It was total luxury listening to her, and if it wasn't for Jenni leaving four missed calls on the Motorola I might not have bothered going out at all. I paid special attention to kissing and cuddling Mam in case it was the last time I ever saw her, then I made a dash out the house because it was getting late late late.

Me and Jenni had another bottle of poppers from the

adult shop, and by the time it got to seven I was seeing a yellow spot. We walked around with that hot feeling in our skulls, laughing at nothing. Jenni looked like a Simpson. It was frosty out, and we tried to keep high snuggling the liquid gold in our mitts. The rest of the girls met us by the crossing, and we shared round the nitrate giggling at each other's clothes. Rachel broke the rules, coming out in a mini-skirt and a very booby top – she was cruising for a spiking. Despite the yellow vision, I sniffed up another full breath on the way to the bus stop, and I started blinking red and green and all the other colours of the rainbow. We were shivering so we got the 27A from Keith Road rather than trekking to Belle Vue, plus it could be crazy and scary down there at that time and we were innocent girls. Speaking of which, Claire had been on the phone that afternoon with the Baby Boy – she wasn't intending on going back to school any time soon, but I said I'd come over in a day or two. Mam reckoned she was throwing her future away having the kid, but I guess you've just got to make the best you can with whatever you have. Claire was never that good at maths, but she'd be a super mam.

You trying to pull tonight? Debbie asked Rach, and we all creased up. I'd come out pretty glamorous too, but I wasn't interested in one- or twoish-night stands any more – sure you get that rush of having a good fuck and you get to pretend you care about someone for a bit, but I hated the feeling of not really giving a shit about any of them. The worst ones were those I was embarrassed about Mam or Natasha or Laura seeing in the morning. Those ones always phoned you as well.

Depends if there's any hotties out, Rachel replied. All I

wanted was a relationship with someone kind and caring and non-smoking – Rachel was an idiot if she was only fooling around with Dan. He was wasted on her. We managed not to slip over as we strode past litter and iced-over puddles, but my high-heels were killing already and it was hard not to skid on the dossed concrete. Thank god the bus came then – we were icicles, and a few smackheads were pinching cigarette butts out of the slush as we ducked under the shelter. Me, Jenni, Debbie, Rachel and Gracie were out, but there's no strength in numbers when you're wearing skimpy clothes and you've had your nails done. The bus was empty so we laughed and had a bitch about a few people from school and I got more and more relaxed. I wanted to get monged and forget all the hassle. Jenni wanted to make a popper tab so she took out one of her superkings and dipped it in the bottle, and we looked cool as anything sucking on an unlit ciggy. For thirty seconds the bus got quite trippy and we felt silly and rather exuberant. There were no more yellow spots like.

As per usual we walked first to the Royal Exchange, since the drinks were cheap and there was usually a lot of people from Brackenhoe there. It was pretty scruffy, but me and the girls just stood and bopped around and it was our kind of music. The usual big dickheads were out; the boys who weave their way into your circle and stare at you like you'll drop everything and get off with them. We looked at each other and laughed our faces off. Contrary to popular belief sometimes girls just want to have fun with their friends, not get hounded by idiots and nonces. We took it in turns to get drinks, and we were starting to feel quite wrecked. Now and then we took drags off the popper tab, and I got another head full of sunshine – thank heavens no one offered to light it.

Boys were dogs. They all wanted to pump their big sloppy dicks inside you then not see you ever again, and try it on with someone else. Girls on the other hand were more sophisticated and mature, and I walked arm in arm with Debbie to get more mortalled. We spotted Abi Ellis coming over, and we bobbed our heads so we wouldn't have to talk to her. I never liked Abi but to her face I was always friendly enough – she used to come to Rachel's birthday barbecues when we were in Beechwood Juniors, and nowadays she was quite the school bitch. However, I had no respect for anyone who got their miaow out all the time for boys on the playground, even if they were only six years old at the time. I didn't feel particularly racist towards her, after all Debbie was the blackest girl this side of Saltersgill field – in fact me and Deb were probably just jealous of her blowjob lips and tanning. Abi wasn't even half-caste anyway – I think she was quarter Spanish or something like that.

What you drinking? I asked Debbie, just for the sake of saying something. I still had loads of Dad's twenty left, and we decided to get tanked up on cherry vodka. We stood and slurped and stared on at Abi, our faces set in that position you get from ponytailing too tight.

God look who's here, Debbie said suddenly. We clocked that poor boy Adam stood nearby cuddling a pint of Carling. He had on this maroony shirt which actually complimented his blotchy scars, and I was impressed. I decided to go over and say hello – I hadn't seen him much since Christmas, and you had to have a soft spot for him even if he was a bit dreary.

Hey, how you doing? I asked, looking him in the eye. He seemed very awkward, and I wasn't sure if it was because he liked me or because he didn't. I felt like I'd been a bit of a bitch to him, but I couldn't put my finger on it. I did like him.

Not too bad, he replied. You having a good night?

It was only just kicking off really – I wasn't half as wrecked as I wanted to be. I flicked my hair back and said, Yeah, it's okay. Who you out with?

He pointed at Abi. Adam was nothing like her – he was shy and super-sensitive; the kind of boy who'd be perfect for you if only he wasn't a fruitcake. A few times I'd caught him opening and shutting things over and over, such as his pencil-case and pack-lunch boxes. For all I knew he could've been a psycho, but I think he was just nervous around people and wasn't dead sure how to hold himself. A sheltered child. I downed the rest of the vodka and went to him, Are youse an item then?

Naw. While we talked I watched him fiddle with his scabs and get a bit twitchy, bless him. I suppose I was that gorgeous though, I sometimes had that effect on boys. I tried to calm him down, but stroking his cheek just made it worse and I asked, You're not still bothered about Gaz, are you?

He backed away slightly like I was going to whack him in the head. I couldn't understand why some people were like that – it was like all he wanted to do was hide in a seashell all the time. If I was him I'd get myself a girlfriend and have a bit of fun in my life for a change. I pushed my dimples out and added, Don't worry about him. He's a dick.

But then he went and spoiled it all and took a cigarette off Abi. It was obvious he was trying to impress me, but with my mam bleeding her lungs out back home the worst way to get into my knickers was smoking. I got a bit pissed off then, like he'd let me down but in the end I wasn't that fussed and I said, How long you been smoking, you bad boy?

Aw, about six month. On and off, you know.

I nodded and decided to get another drink. He was an idiot. You'd think after six month he'd at least learnt how to inhale it – even I knew that. I spent more money on Aftershock and lemon-lime vodkas – it was time to get off my face and not talk to smokers. I began to cheer up once Abi and Adam swanned off, and me and the girls danced as the drinks began to kaleidoscope inside us. Deep down in my heart I knew I'd embarrass myself, but I kept on downing the bevvies and just not worrying about a thing. I wasn't sure if I'd had it completely with boys, but they were very irritating. This lad called Ben came up to us – the same Ben that cheated on me at Empire, though he was incredibly scrumptious and still good mates with Gracie. He used to babysit her. It was hard to take him 100 per cent serious, but he had a few Ferrari pills and I borrowed one off him and necked it down. We continued to use the popper tab. It was madness! Floating around the dry-ice looked all patterned like a magic carpet, and the people were all funny and glowing around us. The night was a fireball. Me and Ben chatted for a short while – I never realised he took pills, and we raved for a bit about them. I tended to get the hots for any boy with free Es, but still in the back of my head they were all shits and it was only one tiny tablet. I wasn't that loved-up. At one point I almost wanted to find Adam and tell him about my mam and the cancer – more than anything I didn't want anyone to smoke themself to an early grave, but I was coming up and I didn't want to talk to him on narcotics. He was strange and I was an angel.

At the end of the night we strolled to Pizza 2000, everyone bored and knackered except me and Benny. I stumbled about on rollerskates. A few other lads who'd latched on to us followed us past Fresco, and I held hands with Ben but I definitely wasn't going to get off with him. A few times my bum got felt but I didn't say anything. I needed a sit-down, and the whole pizza shop was stuttering before my eyes. You could tell we were on something. I declined another popper tab Jenni made with her second-last cigarette. I felt unusual, this spitty stuff leaking into my cheeks, and I asked around for water but there were just doughs and doner meat. It looked like all of us had paired up – Ben was trying to get dirty with my bare thighs, and Debbie and Gracie were both getting stuck into some boys from the street. Jenni was getting poppered up with some freak from the Ex, and they giggled their heads off and I thought they were pretty foolish. Rachel was the only one looking lonely on the benches, but then again she looked lovely.

We laid about. I'd gone overboard. And the night was a cyclone. When the food came Debbie let us steal some strips of doner meat, but on the doves me and Ben had to decline and in any case the garlic dip looked a bit like a man's cum. Ben smuggled in a few cans of Stella, and he cracked one open while taxis and police cars bombed past outside. I was trying not to gurn, that bunny-face being the only nuisance about taking pills for a pretty girl. I was more spaced-out than supercharged though, and I smiled and rested my head on Ben's shoulder. He said I could share a bit of Stella with him, but it was a bad idea. I guess I just wasn't the antisocial type. I nearly hurled as I gulped it – that yeasty taste always reminded me of a sick science experiment, and the last thing I wanted to think about was Brackenhoe. The mix of alcohol and class As sometimes had its drawbacks, and I started getting juddery. I wanted my ducks bed cover, and I whispered to Ben, I think I'd better go home.

And that's when I realised my keys were missing. I clawed through the glitter bag all exasperated and dizzy, everything going wrong around me. I couldn't remember putting them anywhere silly, but it was only a few months back I lost my purse in Zantia and everything got stolen. I almost weeped as I rummaged round the benches for something metal and shiny, but there were just old takeaway wrappers. My teeth felt soft and I was in agony. I wanted a glass of water. My belly killed, and I looked at Ben and he said to me, You can come back to mine if you want.

I just wasn't in that place though. I blew him off slightly, then I had to go outside and make a phone call. I figured Natasha or Laura might still be awake, or as a last resort Fairhurst or someone would be able to give me a lift. In fact Fairhurst was always pretty caring and I thought about phoning him first, and I wondered why I dumped him in the first place. And that's when I realised my phone was missing. And that's when I started being sick.

Toast, tea, chicken fried rice, half bag of prawn crackers, lemonade, popper taste, double vodka-Red Bull, cherry vodka, one blue Aftershock, a few Bacardi Breezers, lemon-lime vodkas, Ferrari, sip of Ben's Stella. All of that as I staggered down Wilson Street.

Chapter Fourteen

Black Lungs Two

Streetlights

Abi Ellis had a habit of stirring shit. The last thing she said to Adam before they got split up was, 'I hate Eve. She's up her own arse; you're miles too good for her.'

It was the last thing he wanted to hear. You know how drones do what they can to get laid by the queen bee, that was sort of how Adam saw Eve. He completely wanted to buzz off her. It took Eve ages to realise Adam even existed, but he was nice and it was quite like Eve to go round with her head in the clouds. Or up her own arse, or whatever. But she didn't exactly have it easy – her mam was dying of lung cancer, and at that very moment Eve was spewing up outside the Pizza 2000. She was in a sad mood – she lost her keys and her phone, and she didn't know what she was going to do. She wandered aimlessly round Wilson Street, blurry eyes, and at about 1:35 she spotted Adam walking around in the swarm of people. He wasn't her best mate, but in times of crisis you tend to grab on to any old friendly face.

'Eve, are you alright?' he asked her, but he could see pretty clear the tears and the zig-zaggy mascara. All she could do was put her arms around him. Tons of cars and people and police-people were charging past at a hundred miles an hour, but Adam kept a tight hold and he knew deep down they were good enough for each other. Eve was looking for the kind, sensitive type and there you had it.

'Will you help me find my keys?' she wept, looking really down but cute in our pink and yellow light. Adam held her hand as they scoured the pavement, though it seemed a bit of a long shot. All they could see was rubbish and empty spaces and blinding glow. Adam so desperately wanted to help her though. They scuttled down back alleys Eve hadn't even walked down before, and the more she got exasperated the more Adam wanted to hug her to pieces – maybe he could smell the sicky smell in her hair, maybe he couldn't. Eve stared up at him with flying saucer eyes and Adam wanted absolutely everything for her.

But he couldn't do a thing. Eve was crying and the keys weren't getting any easier to find. She kept a hold of his maroony shirt, but she didn't want him taking advantage of her and she felt vulnerable with such a spinning-top head. And the pills. Adam was taking special care not to touch her anywhere dangerous, but she couldn't even tell. She sighed and cried more and more. She had to admit it, 'We're not gonna find them.'

'We will,' Adam said, but he was drunk and what did he know. All he wanted was to comfort her, not so much get off with her or get into bed with her. He was pretty perfect for her, but Eve never really went for boys like that – she went for boys who mess you about and don't telephone you and touch other girls' boobs. Adam was trying to keep her warm stroking her arms and wiping her tears, but all she could say was, 'We won't. They're not here, they're not here.'

'We will.'

'If you find them,' she sniffed, 'I'll love you for ever, but if you don't find them I'm just gonna hate you because you lied.'

It was a horrible situation. Eve was getting wound-up, and she let go of Adam's hand and stomped up the steps of Bar Fresco. As she sat down Adam had visions of the keys turning up and the two of them going out and getting married and having beautiful babies, and he was just as exhausted as Eve. At one point he felt Abi Ellis phoning him in his trousers, but he ignored it. As she sat there all swept up in tears, Adam watched disco lights gang up round Eve's head and she looked like a fairy wearing a tiara. He had her on a fine thread and he didn't want to lose her.

'Where did you last have them?' Adam asked softly, perching next to her on the step. She explained about the pizza shop but she couldn't really remember having them there either, and the idea of someone stealing them kept crossing her mind but it frustrated her too much. She hunched her back over her knees and cried black lines, and for once it didn't matter to her when Adam put his arm round her shoulder. It was all he could really do. She sunk her head between her thighs and mumbled, 'My phone's gone too.'

Adam caressed the sky-blue dress, his mind absolutely tortured and all the girl could say was things like, 'And my mam's going to hate me.'

Adam looked out across the crossroads. All the bars and drunk kids met in swirly multicolour, but he didn't dare hail one of the taxis and take her back to his. He was too much of a gentleman, or not enough of one. In the end they decided to walk back to the pizza shop – the last resort. Eve knew for a fact she wouldn't find her things, but what she needed now was her friends and not a complete stranger. Adam sort of read the signs and didn't touch her again. They found Rachel and Debbie and Ben and everyone in the same formation in Pizza 2000, and Eve got a ton of attention – it was obvious she'd been crying. There was a runny nose involved. Adam ended up with his back to the counter. With her friends Eve could speak a lot clearer – Debbie hugged her and said it'd be alright and Ben even made her laugh for a bit. She blew into a Kleenex. Adam and Eve felt completely shit for different reasons. Everyone huddled round, and a couple of boys took the opportunity to touch her up disguised as affection. Adam didn't have the guts to go anywhere near her, but whenever someone looked over he had a sympathetic face so they knew he was sound. He read a text about Abi going home in a taxi on her own and whether he was okay, but he wasn't sure.

'Don't cry, look, it's here,' the boy Ben said out of the blue, holding Eve's Motorola before getting absolutely swamped by her and the sky blue dress. Adam tried not to notice as they cuddled and sat down again, and Ben whispered in her ear, 'Don't worry about your keys, it'll be okay. We'll get some new ones cut tomorrow. Come sleep at mine tonight; you'll be alright.'

And she didn't just sleep at Ben's.

Chapter Fifteen

You Had to Fall for Dynamite

Adam

I could've killed him. I borrowed a kung fu book and a box-ing book from Easterside library, and to warm up I shadow-boxed Ben to death every night. I would like to see Gaz's neck broken and Ben's cock ripped off. It was exhausting, and after a minute I laid on my bed with my head against the brick side of the wall. The wires in my brain were a bit mish-mashed, but then again they always had been. Any sane per-son would've sought out professional help. I looked up. Dad plastered the hole in my ceiling just after Christmas, but if you caught it in the right light you could still see the mark. I wondered if he'd chucked out the *Razzle* as well. Every now and then he seemed weird and suspicious around me, but nowadays the grunts and groans in my bedroom were just me building myself up. The exercise made me sick though – I was so unfit. It'd been about a week since I'd even left the house, but there was no place in Boro for a brittle lit-tle fanny anyway. I hated boys and I hated girls. Instead of happy Beatles ditties I dusted off Dad's selection of darker sixties stuff – *Aftermath* was a good one, Mick Jagger singing all about stupid girls and what have you. Another hot pick was 'The End', the Doors song where Jim wants to kill his father and do other nasty things. I wondered in the world how people got by without ever being sad – there's so many shit things that can happen to you. I lurked about the house with a negative face, sometimes reading the books or playing guitar but none of the hand positions like Tiger Paw or Snake Fist worked too good on the telecaster. Often I cranked the distortion to eleven, trying to cover the feedback at the start of 'I Feel Fine' but the song itself was miles too tricky. I felt shit anyhow – guitar fuzz was a better outlet for those feelings than sweet luxurious songs or dead disciplined martial arts. With the amp that loud all you could hear was squeaking whines and the undercurrent of rumbly bass stuff – it almost gave you a hard-on, music can do that occasionally. I fingered a few chords but in the end I just had to sit back and float around on the sound – the feedback was a flapping bird and a tidal wave, and the sheer volume was like getting drowned in ever so deep water. I could see the great barrier reef. And I held my breath.

Sitting there, the guitar pressed to the amp and me falling down a waterfall, I'd sort of forgotten my mum and dad were home from work. For days I'd been sitting around whingeing to myself about girls, and whatever my Submarine clock said I couldn't really trust it. I was thinking a million suicides when my dad stormed in. He caught me off guard, appearing in all that intense noise.

'Fucking *hell*, son,' he said, with such frowny eyes and red cheeks. He stamped across the carpet and, I guess without really thinking, threw the guitar off my lap and pushed me hard against the wall. Just to be ignorant I struck the high strings and watched Dad's face crease as the amp screeched its head off – he went absolutely mad and smacked me across the face, right where Gaz had caught me a month or so before and I almost felt the jaw buckle again.

'Fuck off!' I yelled. After all I'd made a promise not to take shit off anyone ever again. I tried to remember some of the moves in the Bruce Lee book, but in the end I just lifted the fake Fender off my bed and slung it across my dad's head. I tried to render him immobile by clattering it across his temples a few extra times, and he ended up unconscious and seeping blood. I shit myself then. He wasn't moving, and I jumped from the mattress and tried to sit him up but there was no response at all. I wasn't sure where to look for a pulse and I couldn't hear any breaths. He started staining my carpet. I stood for a while in complete silence, though the amp was still fizzing slightly and I liked the sound of it. Outside my mother was chaining her Mayfairs in the Greggs outfit, and I couldn't be bothered shouting her out the window so I took the Nokia and dialled in 999. It was my first time phoning that number; I wasn't that sure how to conduct myself. I wanted to get my dad out of my room pretty quickly, and while I waited for an ambulance I pretended to kick his head and belly in just for the fun of it. The siren reminded me of feedback.

Eve

I met the Baby Boy the following Saturday. I was never that fussed about little kids even though I enjoyed babysitting Nicole next-door, but I figured Claire would be going through all the post-natal depression stuff and it'd be a laugh sleeping over at hers. None of us had really seen her since the baby was born – it was pretty cruel to isolate her like that, but we all had the mock exams coming up and it was tough getting to and from Park End on a weeknight. I was getting my period the night she phoned – usually I'd make up some shit excuse, but there was nothing on telly and Claire won me over with the mention of pizza and the top and tail. It was harder being her than being me after all – on top of the Baby Boy, she'd split up with Shane and her life was going down the plughole. All I had to worry about was daft lads and come-downs. As of that week, I'd kicked pills for a bit – the night I lost my keys was a bit of a downer, and I was sick of feeling icky and fluey all the time. I wished I hadn't let down my Mam and I wished I hadn't partied with Ben. It was nice for a change being sober with Claire, as long as it didn't involve changing any dirty nappies.

I perched myself on the plastic bench and watched rain drag down the shelter for about twenty minutes, until the 36 or something came with Park End on the front of it. I sighed and dribbled myself inside – the bus was absolutely packed, you had hardly enough room to stand up. Rubbing my nose, I climbed into the luggage compartment and plonked myself down, remembering to bring my knees to chest so as to ease the period pain. We learnt that with Miss Gerard. I felt pretty shit and tired, and I rocked with the bus in the tiny little luggage space. Me and Jenni used to sit there on our way home from town when we were pissed, back when we had to be in before midnight. Back when we lived in adjoining terraces, and back when we were best buds and would never cheat on each other or bitch or be nasty.

Are you alright there, pet? an oldish woman asked me, stood nearby with her kids or her grandkids. I nodded, though there was a wet patch sprouting under my bum getting me all shivery. I wondered if I'd stand up with two dark blue buttocks, but I didn't mind. People tended to look at my bum anyway. After a while, the cramps in my womb started trickling to my legs, and it was a relief stepping off the bus and stretching them up Overdale Road. It felt a lot chillier when I got off, but I was glad the rain had stopped – that steamy bus was giving me a fucking cold. I felt a bit delirious going down Claire's back alley, like tripping off pills that time but not half as happy. The weekends were crazy – Ben had been texting me a bit since the pizza shop episode, but I was partly ignoring him and not giving him the green light – I still wasn't completely in the mood for another boyfriend. Up in Claire's bedroom I told her, I just sort of wish me and Fairhurst were back together. I didn't even realise how good he was to me.

But I didn't like to moan and groan about boys to her. It felt weird watching her answer the door with the baby on the other side of her belly, but she was looking good. She had on a red Dangermouse T-shirt and tight-fit Levis – there was no more need for drawstring trousers and track-ies. I kicked off my trainers then followed Claire into the kitchen, where her step-dad was scrubbing dog-shit off her little brother's shoes. His cheeks were dead pink and angry, but he still span round and winked at me when we hit the lino.

Dave, can me and Eve have the telly in my room for a bit? Claire asked, standing next to him and stroking his arm in the provocative manner. Do you wanna come and move it for us?

Dave stopped what he was doing for a moment, then wiped his forehead and said sharply, Fucking hell, get Joe to do it – I've only got two hands.

Sighing for effect, Claire hummed then brushed past me

into the lounge, being a right drama queen. I followed her and the baby into the purple lounge, then watched as her older brother Joe unplugged the TV and carried it up for us. I recognised him from big school, but he hardly even looked at me as he set everything up in Claire's room and I couldn't be bothered trying to chat him up. I'd had it with boys, hadn't I.

Do you want to hold him? Claire asked, passing me the Baby Boy as Joe charged back downstairs. The little fellow was sleeping, and I paraded him round the bedroom while me and Claire started chit-chatting. She had a cot and other stuff set up in her room, but she still had all her clothes and everything chucked over the floor, and I wondered how she coped in that mess. I kicked a trail to the window and jiggled the Baby Boy above the garden, where little Shaun was running around in his socks. I ended up shutting the curtains though because the sun going down was such a terrible sight.

So how's everyone else? Claire asked, clicking on the television but there wasn't really much on it. I told her a bit about Rachel getting friendly with Dan and the usual stuff about snogs and shags – with Claire you could talk totally freely about the shape of boys' knobs and getting squirted on, but the biggest news was still her having the baby. With all the talking he ended up crying his face off and I passed him back to Claire, but there was no surefire way of getting these things to stop. In the end Claire had to burp him about twenty times, and I popped downstairs to put on the pizza because he was rather annoying. I couldn't believe Claire had to take care of him the rest of her life – it really put you off getting one of your own. I talked for a while with Claire's step-dad in the kitchen, and he kept touching my arm which I didn't like – he either fancied me or was trying to get dog-muck all over me.

Do you think Claire'll come back to school? I asked, just trying to be polite while the oven warmed up.

I dunno. I don't think she wants to, Dave explained, touching me again. I don't think anyone could babysit the Baby Boy anyway.

It was a real shame hearing it put that blunt, and I walked back upstairs to the sound of TV and crying. The Baby Boy was back in his cot when I came in, but he didn't seem to want sleepy-peeps. Claire looked shattered – it was a full-time job having a baby, so no wonder she couldn't go back to school. I tried to cheer her up while we chewed through the Margherita, talking about anything but little kids – boys, periods, sex, class As, Brackenhoe, all the classic stuff, but it probably reminded her of everything she'd lost. Claire wasn't all that depressed but for the rest of the night the baby kept crying and whining, and I got sick of it pretty quick. You wanted to strangle it. I wondered how I'd cope if I had a kid – I supposed Mam would help me out a lot compared to Claire's mam, who tended to work dead late at the Blue Bell garage and Dave didn't seem too much into babysitting. I sighed and munched into the crust.

Your mam working tonight? I asked, as a door whammed downstairs. It was Joe going out, and the baby stirred then let out a stupid noise.

Yeah, she's back about twelve. But hopefully he'll of gone to Nod by then, Claire said, stepping up to the cot and rocking it gently. I finished off the last slice and stacked our plates by Claire's bed, where loads of neglected cats and dogs and dinosaurs stared out. The night was going so slow you sort of wished we had some cider to keep us going, but I doubted Claire was allowed to drink in front of the baby and there was a chance it'd just bring us down.

Are you coming to Rachel's party next week? I asked, licking the bits of tomato off my fingers.

Nah, I don't think so, Claire went. Her face dropped, and for one night I wished she could let her hair down. It was only a few days til Rachel's mam and dad were off to Antigua, and the party would be amazing. But the baby had sucked all the life out of Claire. And I feared the worst when I asked her, You're still up for Majorca though, aren't you?

Claire cringed when I mentioned it – it was such a terrible blow. She glanced where the Baby Boy was gurgling its head off, then said, I forgot to say. I can't. I'll have to stay with him. It's annoying as fuck, but it's just money and that. Maybe one of the others would be up for it?

I pulled a dead sympathetic face, but it wouldn't be the same. Sometimes Gracie and Jenni could be irritating cunts. I sulked, but I sulked for Claire. She got the Baby Boy out of the cot just for the sake of it, and we swapped him about while night completely fell outside. The TV started to flash its colour round the walls, but we had to stick the sound down and there was still fuck-all on it. The baby grabbed at thin air as Claire asked after my mam, how she was doing after the therapy and everything like that. It was always sad getting into that, but she was doing alright. We'd been on a few day trips together, shopping in Newcastle and we did the ice-skating in Boro the week before, and slowly it dawned on me Mam could maybe take Claire's place in Majorca. After all she deserved a holiday, and there was a chance I'd feel crap anyway away from home if she wasn't there. Ever since the cancer I never argued with her and I never wasted any precious moments. All at once there was a nice feeling in my belly, and it wasn't just the pizza digesting and it definitely wasn't the period. Me and Claire and the Baby Boy laid back on the bed covers, watching the smooth ceiling instead of the clutter. I let the baby grab my little finger, and for once he seemed quite settled.

We should set him up with little Nicole, I laughed, imagining the tiny tots dressed in wedding gear and I snorted. It was pretty obvious by now that babies were a total nightmare, but Claire grinned and kissed the thing's teeny forehead. I wondered yet if the baby had been christened or confirmed or whatever you called it, but Claire probably wanted him blown up. She hadn't even named him yet. I still had my heart set on Sydney for a boy or a girl, but I didn't mention it to her because she'd only want it for the devil child. We bounced the kid up and down then switched off the telly – it was getting lateish, and he was starting to get excited and grouchy again. When he screwed his face up he was the ugliest piece of shit, but I didn't say anything. We tucked him up in the Duck Tales cot, then started to get tired ourselves and began getting ready for bed. It was sort of a last-minute thing to have the sleep-over so I hadn't brought any stuff with me; Claire lent me her toothbrush and a tiny Garfield vest, and I managed to change my tampon in the bathroom without embarrassing myself. It was only half-ten when we got in the top-and-tail position, both of us completely sober while the baby dropped off in the corner. Boy had the sleep-overs changed lately. We took a risk and chatted whispers in the dark; every now and then the Baby Boy wriggled about in his cot and we had to shut up, but you couldn't just lay there in silence.

So you really wanna get back with Fairhurst? Claire asked me, hogging the covers but I wasn't fussed. That period was hotting me up.

I dunno. I've just been with too many crap lads recently, I said, for example the sex with Ben the previous weekend was awkward and ever so slightly painful, him not quite being able to heat me up correctly. I mean, the more people you sleep with the more you realise how good you had it before. And Fairhurst only treated me bad that one time, fondling Rachel's perfecto titty, and he phoned me all the time after it happened.

Yeah, I know the feeling, Claire whispered. I wish Gaz would have me back.

You don't mean Shane? I said, raising an eyebrow her toes didn't catch. I rolled over. I always thought Shane and Claire were good together – like me and Fairhurst, their two-year affair had loads of ups and downs but those boys taught us how to have a good time. I thought it was pretty weird her mentioning Gaz – there was a boy I hated right now.

No, I mean Gary Clinton, Claire repeated. Don't tell anyone – it's his baby.

I took some of the covers back, and I hid under them.

Chapter Sixteen

The Lightning

Eve

Fairhurst was at Rachel's party, and I tried to get back with him. But it was hard work – perhaps if I was loved-up I could've slid up to him and said something nice, but in the end I got mortalled. Me and Jenni went halves on six litres of White Lightning, and there was total frost underfoot and we skidded about while we drank it. The cider was knacking my head by the time we got to Fremantle Crescent, a few motorbike gangs buzzing around as we stood by her front door. Rachel had on her red cheer-leader jacket – it was bitter as well indoors, and me and Jen huddled in our coats while we finished the first bottle. Rachel said the pilot light had blown out so there were no radiators, and she had no idea how to fix it. We could see our breath like we were in the *Exorcist* and it was spooky. We made our way through the hall and said hellos to a few people. As I started getting pissed I felt quite high but it was more wobbly than ecstatic. Me, Debbie and Rach sat around nattering about Majorca – Jenni didn't seem all that bitchy and jealous about the trip, and we swore we'd bring her back some tiny Smirnoffs and Baileys off the aeroplane. She sat on the carpet while I perched on the chair arm next to Debbie – the living room was pretty packed with faces, and that's when I spotted Chris Fairhurst.

I felt like I made a dick out of myself. He was laid quite bored-looking on the sofa, and I did my biggest grin but it seemed to go right through him. My head was swirling – I couldn't decide if he'd seen me or not, so I got up and trudged over the people. There were loads of unfamiliar faces, tearaways, and scruffy girls I didn't know too well. I touched their heads til I got to Fairhurst, and I plonked myself down. He just looked at me with pin-point pupils, and in my head I knew I had to be cool but the cider was a bit of a nightmare. I ended up talking to him about the Citroën he crashed, and straight away I could tell I was pissing him off. The last time I saw him was at the traffic lights with Jenni. Then I started fumbling my words, trying to explain the holiday, but he couldn't tell what I was on about. He seemed so cold and lifeless, or he had a new girlfriend or something. I wished I wasn't so drunk – I was aware of making a fool out of myself, but I didn't know how to combat it. I staggered back to the girls, knocking glasses and people's knees, and I sat back down all annoyed and fidgety. I hadn't been this pissed for at least a week. I had the feeling I'd cry about it in the morning, but for the time being there was no reason to sit around worrying about stuff. Fairhurst could do what he wanted.

Me and Jenni lounged around and quaffed more White Lightning – it was so sour and it always made me think of cat poo, but soon enough I was talking shite again and me and Jen floated around with light heads. I kept glancing over at Fairhurst, and I wondered why he was being such a robot. My head was in a muddle about how good looking he was, but there was no denying those cheekbones and green meadow eyes. In a little bit Brandon came in and sat with Debbie, and he blocked my view – those two were having a lover's tiff, but I managed to change the subject. Brandon wasn't so het up when we started discussing bikinis and sun lotion, and I steered clear of holiday romance. We weren't exactly going to Majorca to shag every lad there, but it'd be good to unwind for a week. I was looking forward to coming home roasted.

You alright for drink? Brandon asked me, offering a can of Tennents or whatever it was. I showed him the big bottle of cider and we laughed. I took a can anyway. Brandon was a hotty – at first it seemed weird for Debbie to be going out with a Paki, but he was one of those with nice bracelets and trendy lines shaved into his hair. I wriggled on the hard settee, and I started getting jealous of all the girls sitting around with their boyfriends. Opposite me Rachel and Dan were sloshing tongues, and even Debbie and Brandon necked now and then despite the arguing. Me and Jenni were just the sad cases getting drunker and drunker. I smiled at Dan, then spotted Gary Clinton squashed underneath them slurping up a bottle of Three Hammers. I didn't want him to notice me; I was still cross about him battering Adam as well as putting a bun in Claire's oven. He changed my mood – I bobbed my head back, and I could feel my eyes swimming out of their sockets.

Eve you're wrecked, Rachel went, cradling Dan's hand and laughing. People who say that to you are boring knobs though. She hadn't been drinking much, just sharing a cup of Spectra with Dan and that was that. She seemed pretty happy though – house parties tended to be disastrous, especially with the open-door policy. Sometimes you got people coming in off the street and stealing things, but at least all the thugs at Rachel's were smiley thugs. To me they were all just a bunch of spinning faces. Me and Jenni polished off the rest of the White Lightning, looking really terrible but we didn't give a hoot. Me and her at least wanted to have a good time. I was starting to wish Jenni could come with us to Majorca, but it'd be a kick in the teeth for my mam. And her tits looked really out of shape in her tight Nike top, and in a way I didn't want to witness her in a bikini. Boys still went for her though, for example Ben getting off with her at Empire way before me and him did the squelch. The sex was nothing to scream about though – I think when you start getting laid you imagine boys to have really different styles and ornate techniques, but to be honest they're all quite similar and it's hard even to tell the difference between knobs sometimes. It's safe to say Fairhurst was my best shag, lots of doggy style and licking out and kissing and cuddling afterwards. But now he didn't want to go near me.

Crossing my legs, I felt my tummy churn a bit of cider and I had to balance feeling drunk and feeling sick. My pulse was pumping a little bit harder, and I felt my cheeks drain. I didn't want to sick up in front of Fairhurst so I made a sharp exit out of the room, sweating like mad to the sound of *Street Fighter II* someone had just put on. With the nasty cider swishing about, I darted up the steep staircase and locked myself in Rachel's bathroom. I turned on the cold tap but the water was disgusting, my belly all tight and scrunched. I admitted to myself I'd feel better if I spewed, but the toilet cover was down so I had to quickly gag into the white sink. I felt ashamed. My puke was mostly liquid with a few yellowy lumps of Mam's fish bake, and it filled half the bowl – you'd think by now I'd realise I couldn't hold my drink. Wiping my mouth, I felt absolutely knackered all of a sudden, and slumped in a crumple on the bathroom floor. I was still drunk, and I felt dippy sticking my fingers down the plug to clear the lumps out. I watched the sick swirl away, and I was so used to the milky acid smell I felt sad. I wanted to go back downstairs like nothing had happened, but my guts were in a twist and I was white as an ice cream. Blinking heavily, I knocked my head off the towel-rail then put my back against the cold radiator. I tried to go to sleep. Eyes shutted, the room was still spinning and all I could think of was spew and cider, teasing myself. I had to push my hand into my waistband to get any kind of comfort, and I tried to focus on Majorca. My head was a whizz of coconuts and monkeys and sunshine. After a bit I managed to drop off, or rather completely pass out on the sticky lino. My brain went blank. Only two more sleeps til Majorca.

Adam

In the end I didn't kill my dad. Instead he got hospitalised for a week, and it was a pain in the arse going with my mum to look at him in a coma. He was boring. Mum didn't report me to the police or anything like that (after all the guitar accidentally fell off the top of my wardrobe), but she kept going on about disowning me and now and then in the house she had crying fits. I did what I could to get out of her way. Abi was still mothering me after the disco inferno, and we went out quite a lot though I didn't tell her about smashing my dad's face in. There was no good way to put it. Every so often we went to the Viking or the Grove with her mum and dad – they always bought us drinks and evenings are a lot funner when you're getting tipsy topsy. Me and Abi could sit and talk about anything, and the nights and days always went by dead fast when she was around. I hadn't been thinking about Eve so much recently, but there was always a little part of me that wished it was her and not Abi. I saw her again at Rachel Shannon's party. In the evening I met Abi near the lane on Saltersgill field, and it was that dark sky with odd sun rays coming through like aliens trying to beam you up. Abi was shivering quite a bit in a turquoisey jumper with her arms across her boobs, and the first thing she said to me was, 'Where you been? I felt like a pro standing there.'

I smiled, but I would've felt shit if something happened to her. The lateness was on account of me getting my hair right – I knew there'd be mint lasses at Rachel's party, and I had to look dashing. I think the trick is to scruff your hair in one single motion – the more you touch it, the shittier it gets. I came out with a head like a treetop. I stroked out a crease in my blue-stripe sweater, then me and Abi carved holes in the frost on our way through Gleneagles. After a bit the sun started to squadge across the council flats, glinting the shiny street and we had to walk with our hands over our eyes. We were well and truly deep in a dodgy estate. When we got to Fremantle Crescent the sky suddenly got darker and more sinisterish, and I had the willies – for all I knew Rachel was about to tell me to fuck off. Through school I'd never really talked to Rachel, but she was the sort of girl even if she slapped you in the head you'd thank her for it. We knocked, and it was actually Dan Williams who answered.

'Now. Howay in,' he said. Apparently he was shagging Rachel, and I imagined if I was in the same position I'd be twenty-four-hour smiles and heartbeat. He was just solemn though, and he passed me a can of Harp as we took off our shoes. It was nippy, and when we got in the front room I hardly recognised anyone. I figured the best medicine would be to neck the lager as quick as possible. Me and Abi plonked ourselves on the carpet but no one really acknowledged us. My feet were totally numb, and I held on to them between sips of Harp. Rachel's house had the smell of stale cigs and there were loads of people sat about passing fags and probably joints, but I never wanted to smoke again. I woke up after the Royal Ex that night with grotty fingers, and it took about 150 washes to get the smell off. I forced a couple of smiles out of Debbie Forrester and Gracie as I rocked on the ground – there was some terrible house music playing, and the vibrations were getting to me. The noise was all bum-bum-bum. I couldn't see Eve anywhere. All the way through Beechwood I was wondering what I'd say to her – probably something dead shy and daft, and she'd never talk to me again. She'd been acting weird since I saw her out, and I wondered how the hell I was going to redeem myself. I felt like every time I opened my mouth there was a shotgun in there and I triggered it off.

'Hey you,' Rachel said suddenly, coming into the room and hugging Abi's neck off. She completely blanked me but I smiled up as the cousins kissed and got up to date – Rachel seemed pretty drunk, but I made sure not to gaze down her bra especially with all those lads around I didn't know. She had on a red cheerleader-type coat, with the zip down, and all I could think of was her and Dan fucking

160

each other's faces off. She was like a Tinseltown goddess, although I never heard of anyone from Beechwood or Easterside getting famous.

While Rachel and Abi talked, I decided to down the rest of the Harp and loosen up then look for more drinks. I had a few pounds spare from dinner that week, but in the kitchen there was a big stock of booze everyone was just helping themselves to. I found Debbie and Jenni Farrell and someone else in there – they were arguing about something or other. I stopped to have an eavesdrop.

'What's up?' I asked after a bit. I scratched my face but I didn't really have scabs any more, just little pink blisters from my dad and Gary Clinton. Debbie looked, then did a screwy smile and said, 'These two won't come to the shop with me.'

'It's fucking freezing,' Jenni went, though she had on a yellow Puffa jacket. She was a slice of toast. 'She's going to Palladium and all. She won't go to Saltersgill cos these jealous girls want to boot her face in.'

'I sprayed their car once,' Debbie said, and she was smirking. She jumped up and down on the lino, then turned to me and asked, 'You wanna come? I'm just going for more Coke and that, for the vodka. It's a bit spicy on its own.'

I pretended to mull it over, but who was I kidding really. I nodded, then followed Debbie out the back door as she smiled and stuck her tongue out at the others. We squeezed past loads of bags of rubbish, then went down the back alley and ended up in the dark on Woodville Avenue. The trees were all swishing like white candy-floss on big Twiglets. We crossed over Keith Road, and as we skidded forwards Debbie went to me, 'I wasn't expecting to see you tonight.'

'Yeah, I know,' I said, watching Debbie's head bob across the green boarded-up flats. 'Abi just phoned us up.'

'Are youse two going out together?'

'Naw, just mates, you know. We sort of clicked after the disco and that.'

'Aw yeah, I forgot about that. Gary's a total prick – don't worry about him,' Debbie said, pushing her dimples out then touching my arm. It was always nice hearing people say that about Gaz – I still hated him, but in a weird way if he hadn't pounced on me Abi might not have introduced me to all this wonder. All the girls were Roman candles splashing joy across the estate. Debbie peered up at me in her cream Ellesse jacket, and for once in my life walking through Grove Hill was total bliss.

'So you got your eyes on a girl, then?' she asked, as we made it to the cracked Palladium buildings. I wasn't sure if she was coming on to me, but I'd seen her necking a half-caste earlier on and I said, 'Not really. I mean, have you seen Eve tonight?'

'I knew you liked her!' Debbie laughed, nudging me as we went through the newsagent door. All the kids were piled outside in technicolour tracksuits, laughing and pestering each other, but me and Debbie were completely invincible.

'She doesn't like me, though,' I said bluntly, as we picked up the Cokes and Debbie couldn't resist another one-ninety-nine Bellabrusco.

'What makes you say that? She reckons you're dead sweet,' Debbie went, and we chased each other round the aisles, looking for a fag lighter for Jenni. It was like chiming bells hearing that come out of her mouth – I wanted to rush back to the party and see her, maybe express my total devotion to her or something like that. I seriously considered picking up some Durex, but she only said I was sweet not the statue of David.

'So do you know where she is, then?' I asked, blinking myself awake.

'Yeah, it's a secret though,' Debbie said, smiling as we made our way to the counter. She held the side of my head, putting her lips on my ear and whispering, 'She spewed in Rachel's bathroom. She's in bed now. She's in a right state.'

'Aww, god,' I said, and because we were talking so much the shop assistant couldn't be bothered IDing us. She bagged up the goods, then Debbie paid with a ten and I took the bottles into the biting wind. The streets out there were blue and grey and silver-blue, and we walked close together on the way back to Fremantle. The streetlights were whizzing cross-hairs and I squinted uncontrollably. Debbie talked a bit about her boyfriend as we scooted past the footprints we made on the way down, but I wasn't that interested in niggers really. All I could think about was Eve. I always thought she was untouchable, but maybe everyone's equal after all. I hoped she was okay.

'So how long you been going out with him?' I asked, meaning the boyfriend. Me and Debbie reached Saltersgill again, and you could just about feel the sleet restarting but we didn't mind. Debbie had been seeing Brandon for about a year and a half, and like all older boys he had a habit of being a dick and spending time with other girls and not phoning her sometimes. We made our way through the frost and mist, and I decided right then my girlfriend would be treated like gold. And her name would be Eve.

'I mean, one time me and Brandy were in Spensleys and these daft black bitches kept coming over,' Debbie went, as we got to Rachel's door. 'He didn't even introduce me as his girlfriend. And they kept trying to kiss him while I stood there.'

'That's shit,' I said, clinking bottles. 'What did you do?'

'Nowt really. He's always at it, though.'

'Aw Debbie, sounds like you're too good for him,' I said, and even though it sounded corny she rubbed my arm and said I was dead lovely. I was still in that high mood like a Christmas tree, and once we got the Bellabrusco going we were giggling and I desperately wanted to find Eve. I felt bad about leaving Abigail in the front room, but when I popped my head in she was surrounded by boys and she seemed to be having an alright time. I left her to it – it was about ten or eleven, and I took a mug of the wine upstairs then realised I had to piss. It was a school night and my mum didn't want me coming home late, but since my dad was in a coma I doubted there was much she could do about it. I was starting to understand there's more to life than pleasing your parents. Going to a beautiful girl's party was like getting a gold ticket for Willy Wonka's factory thing, and I was in a white chocolatey dream as I surged upstairs. It almost didn't register when Gary Clinton burst out of the bathroom door, doing up his jean fly. I hadn't seen him since the disco attack, and I felt the hot freezes go up my spine as I stopped at the top of the landing. Our eyes connected, but all he said to me was, 'Alright mate.'

And things continued to get better and better. With all that shock I nearly forgot how to pee, but I managed a little bit standing in the bathroom and grinning in the mirror.

Gaz wasn't so bad. I didn't look shite either – all the swells and bruises were gone, and even though me and Debbie braced the elements my hair was still in place. It was a black mountain topped with snow. I felt a little unstable though – my feelings were all soaring peaks and valleys, sometimes the sun shone and sometimes it rained rainbows. I struck a little kung fu in the mirror, feeling a bit stronger, then ran the cold tap and cupped some water in my mouth and face. I couldn't work out if I was drunk from the drink or just drunk on love, but I was definitely beaming. I smothered my face in Rachel's teddy-bear towel, then straightened it on the rail. I cleaned the mirror, scratched a bit of a scum-line out of the sink, then tried to finally compose myself in the falling light. It was getting late and there was a sleeping beauty knocking around somewhere. I left the bathroom looking serious, and I didn't really have to shut the door many times. But you could tell I was sloshed, and I made a bit of noise searching round the bedrooms for Eveline. The first one had drooping flower wallpaper, and straight away I clocked a person sat in the bluey dark. There was Rachel knelt by this slim purple mound, and I felt suddenly embarrassed for being such a nosy cunt. She turned on the white carpet and blinked – it was like the sleet had come indoors, and I tried to smile shiny snowflakes.

'Hi, Rachel,' I said, all shaky and lost. 'How is she? Do you want me to look after her for a bit? Don't want you to miss your own party.'

'Are you sure?' she whispered, but she was already standing up. 'She's a bit boring.'

I laughed, and it was nice talking to Rachel too. All the girls were princesses. I glanced for a second at Eve – she had the covers pulled right up to her chin but I saw her blonde hair sprawled all over the bubblegum-light pillow and I felt my heart go bump. I crept past Rachel and her CDs and clothes and special things, and you could hear the heavy breaths. I said to Rachel, 'Yeah, it's fine. You go enjoy yourself. You can trust me – I won't do owt to her.'

And I meant it too. If the Prick was in the same position he'd probably lift the covers, look at a bit of boob, perhaps inspect the knickers. But she meant more to me than just getting a stiffy. Boys were idiots if they just wanted to put their willies in a hole rather than care about someone. I regretted even thinking about those Durex. Rachel giggled and scruffed my hair up, and as she snuck out onto the landing she went, 'She'd probably enjoy it anyway! You should've seen me and Gracie trying to undress her earlier on – pure lesbo.'

I cracked up, then said see you later and sat there with Eve, all gorgeous and quiet. Yawning, I watched the purple duvet rise as she breathed out, and she looked so cute with a strand of saliva across her lipstick. I wriggled on the ground then crossed my legs, wishing I could do something for her. It was our first time properly alone together, but it was an unusual situation – I could've asked her out if only she was alive. I sighed. She was beautiful, and I wanted to memorise every part of her in case we never ever saw each other again. Her hair was like a lightning-strike, eyes spiders, sweety lips, Bondi Beach cheeks and make-up. I scratched my chin then leaned a bit closer to the bedside, tingling as her breath tickled my chops. My heart was going whack-whack-whack and I was in love with her. I could've spent the whole night there, but as Eve's eyes started to part and her blood started rushing round, I had no idea what I was going to say to her.

Eve

It felt like someone dropped a cartoon ton-weight on me. I must've been thinking about Majorca pretty hard – I wasn't sure how long I'd been asleep, but my belly was still churning and my eyelashes were glued. I wiped my mouth then rolled about in the bed – I didn't have a clue where I was, but I figured it was Rachel's room and slowly the memories of the party started to jigsaw themselves together. My skull was absolutely exploding. It was hard to look through the dark, and I got the shock of my life seeing Adam's head by the bedside. Where did he come from? I couldn't remember him being at the party, and I couldn't even speak when he shifted his weight and asked, You okay?

I was feeling fucking groggy. And paranoid – all of a sudden I remembered embarrassing myself in front of Fairhurst; I wondered if he was still around, but I didn't have the energy to get out of the covers. I put back my head and grimaced. My throat was in ribbons from all that throwing up, but something else just didn't feel right. I started to shiver as I realised I was in my bra and knicks, and in between my legs I felt quite sore. I glanced at Adam but he seemed fairly innocent – I wondered if I was dreaming him or if he was really there. He just sat and stared, and I curled up in a little ball with terrible stomach cramps. And that's when I realised my pants were halfway down my thighs, and someone had been at my miaow. Even my bum-hole was a little achey. The panic shot through me like a train-set – I had that distinct feeling of being fucked, and the shock was so intense I had to hold back the tears while Adam just stopped there on the carpet.

What you doing? I mumbled, pulling up the knickers. Thank god I was covered by the duvet – one of my boobs had been squashed out of my bra, although I guessed it was nothing he hadn't seen already.

I've been taking care of you, Adam replied. What a sick way of putting it. I wanted to get rid of him – I couldn't believe what kind of morbid cunt got into bed with unconscious girls. I screamed air as I sat up all rigid, but my head throbbed so much I couldn't really argue with him. I was shuddering – every single position in bed felt like medieval torture.

Where's Rachel? I asked. I couldn't look at him – I bet he felt pretty hot losing his virginity to me, and the more I thought about my miaow the more it started to sting. I didn't have the guts to check it for sludge.

She's downstairs, Adam said, with this fake bunny-wunny voice, But I'll stay with you, if you want.

No, I snapped. Fuck off! Get Rachel . . .

Adam's face totally dropped, but then so did my knickers. It did seem like genuine anguish, and for a second I wondered if it was really possible for him to fuck me without me knowing – he was always so shy and feeble at school. I wished for one moment I wasn't so attractive to boys. Adam shot out the room pretty sharp – even if he felt guilty, what good was that? I figured it was always freaks from schools who did that kind of thing, though – I felt sloppy, full of spew and all violated. And to think I used to really like him.

Rachel came up the stairs after about a minute or so. It was hard to tell if she was drunk – she was smiling a big red wedge and I tried not to weep when I said to her, What did he do to me?

Who; that Adam lad? Rachel asked, raising tweezer eyebrows. Dunno – he's alright isn't he?

I swallowed down the sobs – they tasted just like White Lightning, and I had trouble keeping them down. I touched my belly again, then got shivery again and said, But I'm all undressed . . .

God, you dafty, Rachel smiled, but she could tell I was in a bad way. At last it felt good to have my best friend by my side instead of some strange boy, and I managed to curve a smile when she added, Me and Gracie got you out of your clothes. They're just down there.

Rachel pointed at my blue USA top and denimy trousers by the bedside table, but my eyes were so icky it was hard to focus. I was still dead juddery and tearful, and I went to her again, But I feel like someone's been touching me up.

Rach just laughed, and I had to smirk as well when she said, God, you're absolutely mortalled. Nothing's happened to you! It was me and Gracie – we pretended to feel you up when we got you into bed.

You bitch, I said, but it was a massive relief. I adjusted my knicker bottoms again, and in my head my bits didn't feel so hurty any more. I screwed my eyes then breathed out really loudly – it'd been a mad night, and I was better off getting some kip instead of fretting about stuff. I felt bad chucking Adam out, but he'd get over it. I decided to fill my head back up with sunshine – Rachel tucked me in, and I ended up sleeping at hers. Even though I was sicky and disgusting she jumped in with me, and it was nice having someone close to me again. But not that close.

Chapter Seventeen

Revenge-O!

Claire

Next time I get raped I'm going to have an abortion. I looked shit in the mirror – I was once famous for the ice-blonde hair and sprouting boobs in Year Seven, now everything was just a tip. My eyeballs were in some serious need of a cucumber. Speaking of which, I hadn't seen any action for ages and that green dildo from Ann Summers was hardly getting me off any more. To be honest the idea of getting dicked was quite sickening. Shane dumped me as soon as he realised I was carrying, or at least he stopped coming round and I got the hint. Rumour had it he was seeing Katie K from Berwick Hills now = a complete whore compared to me. But Shane and me both knew the Baby Boy wasn't his, so you couldn't really blame him – Shane always wore a Durex or a Trojan and we were dead careful. And to think I used to say they were a nuisance. In the Duck Tales cot, the baby was making a terrible racket. With him not being able to talk and all, it was impossible to tell if he wanted feeding or changing or whatever else, especially when my mam and Dave were out. I sighed and tried to rock him a little, but he didn't shut up. I pretended to throttle him. There was quite a bit of spew in the side of his cot, but I figured if I cleaned it up he'd only go and dirty it again. He was the absolute devil-child, but what can you do. I went around wearing ear-muffs and stuff. It was half-term that week, but the girls didn't seem to come round any more, and the only sign of any boys on the horizon was Clinton – I couldn't see him changing any nappies, and he did have a habit of raping you, but he was my only chance really of a serious relationship. We used to go out at the start of secondary school, and all I could remember was the carefreeness and the hilarity. We used to climb fences and stamp on people's gardens and laugh at dead animals together. I supposed we'd just tell the Baby Boy he was conceived on a paradise island with 'When a Man Loves a Woman' playing. I sat there and watched the kid go red, bawling, and I was pure bored. I wasn't sure how Clinton felt about me, but I guessed if he was desperate to fuck me nine months ago he'd at least be into going out one night. I decided to give him a bell. 'Hi, Gary. You up to much?' I said when he picked up. 'Naw mate,' Clinton replied, and it was annoying him always calling me his mate. He went on about driving his brother's dodgy new Nova, getting into capers with the police and suchlike, but I could feel the phone bill stacking up and I tried to cut him off. 'So you seeing anyone at the moment?' I asked down the phone. 'Well yeah, sort of,' he replied, and my heart bombed. 'I shagged Eve at Rachel's party.' I went, 'You serious?' but I felt totally squashed. Clinton didn't even get it – he wanted me to hear all the gory details, for instance fucking her in the front and in the behind in Rachel's bed, her legs up by his ears and him coming like a skyrocket, but I was more cross at Eve than him. Eve knew I wanted to get back with him, and it wasn't the first time she'd stolen someone from me. I even caught her giving glad eyes to my brother once. It was pretty typical for Clinton to go getting stuck into a load of different girls but I couldn't hate him, after all he was the only chance of Damien having a daddy. When I got off the phone the house felt emptier and emptier. I was fuming – I shot upstairs to check if the Baby Boy had died, but unfortunately it was there wriggling around and making sound. I picked him up – the thing was horrible, gurgling and clinging on to you like a pink tarantula. I felt like throwing it against the wall, but I was only wound up about Eve. It was merely weeks since we had that sleep-over and I told her I wanted to get back with Clinton – I remembered her saying ages ago she didn't even like him that much. I shimmied the baby's weight in my arms, but I couldn't stand staying in the house – I needed fresh air, and I started getting our coats together. I was sick of that stinky little kid smell, but when we got onto Overdale Road there was a nasty wet breeze and it frustrated me even more. We got drenched. All I could think about as we walked past the health centre was how shit my life had got – I used to have amazing visions of boyfriends and dream jobs and maybe a big house in America. Now I just had stretch marks. Every house I passed all I had on my mind was that spoilt bitch in Beechwood. My head and my lungs and my belly were hollow, and I wanted to go argh! We trudged on – the Baby Boy didn't even have a buggy yet, and god knows who he got the fatty gene from. When we reached the end of Overdale and the rain really started, I forced out a bit of a cry. 'You wanna go see Eve?' I asked him, since we were only a stone's throw from Bitchwood and I had to sort things out with her. The baby didn't say anything, but there

was no point turning back. I ducked his head under mine
and we shot over the beck and the rusty railway line. The
sky was getting to be glorious black-coal cloud and it was
pissing it down. I felt like complete shite – my head was
splitting open as we ran away from the streamers, and quite
possibly I could feel my periods coming back on top of all
that. I walked round the back of the mental hospital,
cradling the Baby Boy all the way to Belle Vue, and it was a
relief as the drizzle fizzled out. Me and the baby were covered in teeny tiny droplets like teddy bears, and we went in
the shop to dry off a short while. I bought us a pack of
Jammie Dodgers, not that the baby had taken to sweets yet
but I was starving. We sat on the bench while I gobbled
them up – it was depressing watching the cars go round and
round the roundabout, but my head felt better. I laid the
Baby Boy on my lap while I worked my way through the
love-hearts, and I dropped crumbs all over him. I didn't
really give a fuck. It looked like torture walking the opposite way to the litter bin, so I left the half-eaten packet on
the bench and me and the baby crossed Keith Road together. I cleaned him up for the sake of keeping up appearances,
though my arms were killing from all that carrying. He was
growing dead fast, and I was only a little girl. When we got
to Eve's I had to drop him by the gate, watching he didn't
roll about while I composed myself. It was a Friday morning and Bitchwood seemed ever so quiet, and all the fallen
leaves got me thinking more and more about Eve. I wanted
to tear her fucking hair out, tell her not to touch Clinton
ever again, and as for being friends she could fuck herself
from now on. Definitely no more sleep-overs. Just to make
a point I blammed really hard on her front door, the Baby

Boy banging its head and trying to crawl as it laid out on the garden. One of Eve's slut-o sisters came to the door in a dressing-gown and went to me, 'You after Eve? She's gone to Majorca this morning. You know, with Rachel and everyone . . .' I almost broke down again. I'd forgotten all about the holiday – another fucking excuse for Eve to sleep around, and my eyes were welling up as I stood in the yard. Her sister could tell I was pissed off, but I couldn't really take it out on her so me and the Baby Boy pulled ourselves together and set off back into the morning glaze. I gave that holiday up because of the baby – what a gift from the stork he was. 'So when they back?' I asked, turning around again. 'Don't know. A fortnight or something like that.' I nodded, but I sulked all the way from Beechwood Avenue to the dingy roundabout, and that's when the weeping began again. First me, then the Baby Boy. I had this amazing urge to throw myself in the middle of the road, and the idea of going home and slitting my wrists was slightly exciting. But I wasn't a sick fucker – I had a lot to live for, if only the baby wasn't dragging me down all the time. I blew out air and we cried into each other's faces. I didn't want to go back to the house straight away – I hated the idea of sitting around in all the chaos and shit and wee again, but the estate didn't have much to offer either. At least there was no one around to see me bawling. We walked on, and my little fingers were frosting over in such a massive gale – I seriously wondered if my eyes would get icy from all the crying. I just kept on looking glum, but the thoughts were killing me. The Baby Boy screwed its face up as we tripped down Belle Vue Grove, the trees all dripping with raindrops and I knew exactly how they felt. Five minutes later we reached the beck again, and we stood at the side of the bridge as the water rose and surged like a black brick road. I watched it cut through the Grove Hill and the Berwick Hills, and I wished I was anywhere but there. I thought of Eve and Rach and Debbie in Majorca, sunning themselves and not giving one care about the people back home. I imagined them fucking a bunch of Spanish hunks, and I was fucking jealous. Eve probably didn't even care about Clinton – she had that special way of using people and getting whatever she wanted. She had it so easy. I leaned on the railing and bobbed my eyes around the silver streets and granite buildings, propping the Baby Boy in one arm as I took out a Sovereign and smoked it. It was my first cigarette since the baby, and my hands shook as I puffed. 'What are we gonna do with you?' I whispered to him, but he didn't know. For a moment he was quiet and I relaxed a minute, til the wind picked up again and the tantrums started over. The noise was incredible – even my mam couldn't get him to shut up sometimes. I threw out the fag then lifted him in two hands = what an ugly idiot he was. My brain was overflowing with babies, boys and bitches, and it fucking knacked. I told Eve it was Clinton's baby, and she still went and shagged him. I knew me and Clinton were over – he always had his eye on a thousand different girls, and he didn't even know the kid was his. He wasn't going to change. I cuddled the little knobhead in my arms for a minute or two, but the crying was unbearable and I really wanted to strangle it. It struck me for the rest of my life I'd only have the Baby Boy for company, and so far he hadn't been much of a mate. I stood him on top of the railing, and we had a dance as the wind eased and we saw a couple of slivers of blue sky. I made a little prayer, then I scrunched my eyes and acciden-tally-on-purpose threw him off the rail. There was a big plop in the water, and a bit of red where he must've smacked off the bottom. I faked a look of horror, Clinton's jaw and my hair colour and cheekbones washing down the dirty stream. I felt a bit sick, but at least I'd got it over with. I didn't want to hang around the scene of the crime too long, so I pushed up my Nike collar and headed back to Park End – I felt like all the estate's eyes were on me, but killing the baby was just a silly mistake. We've all been there. I pushed my lips together and charged down Overdale Road again, the breeze still going but nothing holding me back. When I got in I made sure to phone 999 straight away, and I waited for them to come round with another Sovereign on the go, and a story in my head. I stared at the windows. I felt alright – the sky wasn't exactly glowing, but all the black clouds they were diamonds.

Chapter Eighteen

Flapping Wings

Adam

Abi came round one night looking like a tramp, all dolled up in a magenta miniskirt, but I couldn't really complain. Only I'd been thinking all weekend about Eve and the stuff at Rachel's, and as for other girls I wasn't really noticing them that much. All I could think about was what could've been. Debbie said Eve liked me, but then again it was hard to take 'fuck off' as a come-on. I tried to put myself in Eve's place, absolutely monged and waking up to a strange face – maybe she reacted like that because she didn't want me to see her all dishevelled, or she didn't know who I was. I wasn't sure. Maybe she was on the blob; she seemed pretty angry. But I loved her even more – every evening I cranked up the radio (Dad was still in hospital) and imagined me and her hanging out, spending days in bed, snuggling, being dead caring towards one another. That night I had the Doors on, and the music whizzed around like a whirlybird. I had my eyes shut.

'Oi oi,' Abi said, though I wasn't expecting her to actually burst in my room. 'How's it going?'

'Abi. Alright?' I said, opening them up and noticing her skirt.

'I'm fine me,' she smiled, and she sat on the edge of my

bed as I switched off the CD. It was up to 'Blue Sunday', but in general I wasn't really feeling blue any more. It was a Sunday, though.

'Your mam let me up,' she went on, crossing her legs.

'So, what you up to? You wanting to go out or something?' I watched her lay out on the greyish bed cover, and she sort of had slitty eyes when she said to me, 'I dunno. I thought we could maybe stop in or something – I'm pretty skint. Just felt like seeing you.'

I did a little nod. She did look glammed up – I couldn't work out why she'd done her hair all different, and I shifted around trying to be natural. I hummed for a second not knowing what to say, then I stretched and asked, 'So what you been doing today?'

'Not much,' Abi said, sitting up. 'Done all the History coursework, so at least that's out the way. Just been crap weather, so no point going outside or anything and it's dead boring at home.'

I couldn't argue with that. You spend the whole of school wishing for the holidays, then when you get there you do fuck all with yourself. It was good to relax, but I just wanted to see Eve again. She'd been in my head all the time, like there was a little chair in there and she was sitting on it. I shut the Doors back in the CD case a couple of times then joined Abi on the duvet cover, making sort of sand dunes on the dull fabric. While she talked she kept touching my knee, and she asked if I wanted to put on more music – I didn't though. It's embarrassing getting asked that when you've got slightly weird taste in music. I wasn't sure if she could handle Jim Morrison sexing everything up, or the Byrds getting eight miles high, or even the Beatles wanting to hold your hand. She was more of a cheesy pop tart.

'You getting up to much over half-term?' Abi asked, sitting up straight but every now and then leaning over at me. You could see the tops of her tits peeping out of her vest, but you tried not to look. We were like the corpse and the exotic dancer. I breathed out, flinching whenever she touched me, and I got red the more she flirted around. Was she taking the piss?

'Not really,' I answered eventually. I was so shit talking to her when I was sober, and in the silences it got more and more obvious. She lounged about like a pile of pornography, giggling and trying to rile me up. I wasn't sure what she was getting at – I couldn't see Eve being such a dickhead. Abi flicked her fringe out of her eyes, and I had no idea how to react when she brushed over my knob with her hand. She said oops and watched for my thing getting perky, but my brain was like a ball of string unravelling and I couldn't move. I got in a tangle. I tried to keep her at arm's length, but then she went and opened her legs and I completely lost it. She had on no knickers, and my heart went crash-bang-wallop and my eyes popped out. She hadn't shaved, and her fanny looked like a tropical fish or a bit of old carpet.

'So, you just gonna sit there?' Abi asked, and I laughed nervously. I was hardening up, but it was all a bit of a shock really. All I'd planned that night was listening to a selection of records and maybe some homework. I tried to go down on her, thinking back to the *Razzle* and how the boys did it in that. But my heart wasn't into it – her cunt smelt a bit like an armpit, and when I pulled the lips open I knew I'd have to shut them numerous times or else I'll die of Aids or

I'd fall into it. I sat up again, then huffed out air, pissed off at myself. Abi got the hump, and just to make it worse I said, 'Soz, we should just be mates.'

I couldn't wait to tell Burny and the Prick I'd blown off Abi Ellis, but at the same time I felt shit and the semi-on in my Y-fronts was going nowhere. Abi swung her legs off the bed, then kicked the carpet in her socks and asked, 'You're not even seeing anyone though, are you?'

'Well no,' I went. 'Just feel like I'm getting somewhere with Eve.'

'Fucking hell, she's a bitch. She's been with about twenty different lads since Christmas. She's a total slag.'

I didn't believe her, though – that night in Rachel's bed, all soft and fragile and sleepy, Eve was an innocent kitten. If she was such a slapper she would've had a baby or a disease by now – she just wanted to have fun with her life. Something I knew nothing about. In the end I whacked myself off over Abi, recalling the tropical fish and imagining us riding each other, and I sort of wished I'd lost my virginity instead of being a knob. I chased her down the staircase and a little of the way down Deighton Road, but she wouldn't turn back. So I beat myself off when I got home. And I beat myself up. And I didn't have the balls to phone her.

Eve

We had our heads in the clouds. The plane to Majorca flew off at about six o'clock, and I felt so wasted I thought my brain was weighing us down. I stared as the world fizzled away below us, then tried to stretch my legs but there wasn't enough room with my hand-luggage full of tops and bikinis down there. It was weird sitting next to Debbie and Rachel instead of my sisters, and we couldn't have as much of a laugh with Mam there, but it was fun flicking through magazines while the air hostesses looked after us. We stashed a load of mini Smirnoffs and Gordons and all the other names for Jenni and Claire, and I hoped to god the bleeper wouldn't go off when we walked through customs. I wasn't even positive Claire had had a drink since having the baby, but she deserved it and I figured she'd need a night out when we got back home. Claire was an absolute star coping with a kid as well as that shite with Shane and Gary; I'd hate to be in her shoes. In fact I packed a pair of her stilettos for the holiday, but that was a different story. I pulled my pony-tail through the gap in the back of my Yankees cap, then tried to see England out of the window but it was way too cloudy. I couldn't wait for the sunny sunshine.

Giggling at the problem pages in Debbie's copy of *Sugar*, I finished my dinky can of lemonade then pushed a bit of fringe under my cap when it flapped in my eye. I wasn't in the mood to get pissed just yet after what happened that Thursday – I was sick of hearing how wrecked I was, and the whole mix-up with Adam was just annoying. The morning after I tried to go downstairs and apologise to a couple of people, but I was feeling like death warmed up and neither Adam or Fairhurst had slept over. I hoped it'd all be blown over by the time we got back. That afternoon Jenni and Gracie took the piss out of me at the chippy, even though I bought them each plastic forks. Cheeky bitches. Jenni got off with Ben again at the party, but I didn't care because since the Empire I'd shagged him and she hadn't. I still hadn't found my keys, but Mam got more cut and she didn't really probe me about where I ended up that night. She was pretty cool compared to other people's mams – she said me and the girls could do whatever we liked in Palma, and she wasn't bothered about us being rude on the plane. She was fast asleep. We had to go to the doctor's earlier in the week to check she could go abroad, but apparently she was doing really well cancer-wise. It was a good start to the hols. I wiggled in my seat, then read one of the Agony Aunt things to Debbie – the one about the girl who thought her boyfriend's dick was too big for her. It was a better laugh reading them aloud – because of the dyslexia Debbie reckoned she was dead slow at reading, but I think she was just backward.

Once the hostesses came round with the meals, Thursday was miles out of my head. I'd drink again. We still had hangovers like dull halos, but bad heads are alright in the sunshine and we wouldn't be buying shit cider this time. It'd be all Daiquiris and Blow Jobs et cetera. Within hours we'd be dancing and romancing on the streets of Palma and Magaluf, while everyone else had to suffer another boring night down Easterside. Even though we wanted to go mad every night I made a promise not to spew my guts up every time – I didn't want to wake up thinking I'd been bummed again. I liked all the attention though, even if it was mostly just people taking the mick – in Chipchase Chippy Gracie said I was a 'porno zombie' that night. I'm sure I was a sleeping beauty really.

When the plane came in to land, I could feel my ears crunching so I chewed Orbit while the Mediterranean Sea revolved underneath us, with tiny speedboats leaving white slug-trails in the glitter water. I fidgeted around, looking forward to that blast of oven air you get jumping off a plane – I couldn't believe we were frost-bitten in Teesside only hours earlier. Daydreaming, I watched a bunch of wonky windmills scoot past the windows as the plane touched down on the runway, and I nearly had a heart attack when we boinked off the seats. Everything looked yellow and brown like a 1970s film. I was still a bit shook-up when I picked the clothes bag from between my legs, but it felt brilliant to see the sun out and all the Spanish lads working in the airport. Tiptoeing down the aisle in the pink summery heels, it was good to be a million miles from all the shite I'd left behind.

Chapter Nineteen

Resorts

Eve

We had to queue up the steps of Pacha for about fifteen minutes, but it was nothing like freezing your boobies off in Middlesbrough. It was still fairly bakey in the pitch-black, and we jigged around to the muffled beats instead of standing about with our arms crossed. Scratching the sunburn under my black disco dress, I followed Debbie's eyes out across the harbour and all the dotted hotel lights flicking in front of the palm trees. What beauty. She yawned loudly, swaying her hips – I doubted she was still jet-lagged; it was only an hour time difference or something. Next to me Rachel already looked a bit tanned – we'd been out on the beach a couple of afternoons, but I was only on the Factor 6 so far. I felt pissed, and I couldn't help tripping in my silver high-heels as we made our way to the top of the brown stairs. I lent the shiny metal belt off Rachel, so don't worry I was colour-coordinated. Before Pacha we'd been for some vodkas in a cheapo bar on the seafront, and the measures were like four times what we were expecting and it was taking its toll.

As cars and motorbikes stormed along the Gabriel Roca, I smiled up at the young American bloke doing the tickets, then took a few bright notes out of my purse and handed them over. He winked and passed me back some change, but I supposed it was his job to be flirty so I just said, Gracias.

I pronounced it with a cee; I wasn't into all that lispy nonsense. Half of the club was open-air and it looked gorgeous as we went under the big massive archway, the canopy all pink and orange in the blue night. There were too many oldish foreigners knocking about for my liking, but deep deep on the dancefloor you could see a bunch of sexy Spaniard heartthrobs. There was a hint of feeling you're in a porno though. Flicking the lacy straps along my shoulders, I started beaming as Debbie and Rachel joined me on the paving, but all Deb wanted to do was pick her nails while we waited at the bar. She was still yet to sign her tag in Majorca, but I bet there was a Magic Marker in her bag somewhere. I went for a Bacardi and Coke then handed over a bit more Monopoly money, bopping around getting excited.

Stop messing with your manicure! I smiled at Debbie, though she did have quite an extravagant one. After we'd been sunbathing at Cala Major, Mam paid for us to get our nails done up Jaume II since she knew we were heading off to Pacha and that. For the first few nights she came drinking with us but she said the smoky clubs were too much for her, and I felt bad about leaving her up in the hotel. She wasn't looking too well, but I figured it was nothing the sun couldn't fix. We agreed to keep her company in the daytimes, then get out of our minds when she's not around. I looked at Debbie and Rach and hugged their necks and grinned.

Howay, do you want a dance? Rachel asked, pulling us inside. We pushed the thick double-doors open then shimmied carefully onto the dancefloor; the kick-drum was a heartbeat and I wondered if there was an ecstasy dealer about. However I wasn't keen on the idea of overheating. I held my sequinned bag in two hands while I squeezed past flesh and sliding high-heels, checking out the blokes, and I tried to keep my white nails in the lasers. There were a few fine specimens eyeing us up on the beach that morning, but I doubted they'd happen to be in the club as well. In fact nowadays I was very wary about freaky stalker types, after Adam and whatnot even if he was harmless. The dancefloor was small compared to somewhere like Millennium, and you could really tell we were in a foreign country – it was an eighties time-warp, lads still body-popping with daft curly hairdos. The music was class though, and everyone looked like a Calvin Klein model. Debbie had her hair braided again, and her face lit then ducked as the bubblegummy lights moved. I saw her boobs almost jig out as we squashed through a circle of lads, all crowding around and trying to sleaze us but we weren't interested. I spent the whole of the next song with a sweaty boy's hand on my arse, but I half boogied with it and half tried to get away. Me, Debbie and Rachel stuck together like ballerinas, and I opened and closed my eyelids as all the lights shone down like stardust and snowfall. I really hoped it wasn't freezing for all our friends in Beechwood.

I figured it was the hot weather making the boys that extra bit randy. There were a few Sexy Cunts and Honey Bunnies in the audience but I wasn't sure if I wanted their tongues forced down my gob. Possibly they had rabies. We scooted out the way now and then, and I pouted at Rachel with the strawberry lip-gloss clogging me down – she was getting dry-humped by some monkey, grinning her head off though. I couldn't resist wiggling my bum into another lad's crotch when he took me round the waist, but it was total pot luck as to what he looked like. It turned out he was complete Eurotrash, and when he span me round to get dirty I just had to smile and slope off. Blinking neon through the Spanish mascara, I placed my shiny bag down on the dancefloor then tiptoed round it to some house tune we recognised, trying not to step on the rolling bottles and trying not to die from soaking wetness.

Pacha only started filling up at about three, and soon it got knackering in the scorching heat with all that men's testosterone round our heads. It was a class night, but it was weird not knowing anyone except for Debbie and Rachel – in Middlesbrough you could latch on to twenty-odd mates on a normal night. Yawning slightly, I glanced up at the ceiling and the tangerine fabric hanging down off it, like a glow-in-the-dark version of Doggy market. Christ was I really homesick. Smoothing the blonde plaits down my neck, I flicked my lashes at the girls then led them off the dancefloor since we were completely evaporating. My face was still pretty fresh when I spotted it in the glass reflection, and we pushed open the double-doors then stepped into the cool nighttime. Outside it was hard to tell if the sun was going down or coming up and none of us had on a watch, so I touched Rachel's shoulder and asked, How do you get the time in Spanish?

Rachel was big on her languages, and I giggled when she did the accent and went, El tiempo, por favor?

Smiling berries, I clip-clapped my platforms on the concrete then wandered round the tables and wicker chairs until I caught the beady eye of some bloke by the bar. He

had nice funky sideburns and he winked as soon as we
moved up, although we tried not to give the wrong impression. It felt really late and the drinks were fading off quite a
bit, but I was still laughing when I asked him loudly,
Eltimpo, mon pavor?

Pardon? Sideburns asked, sipping a funny red cocktail. I
didn't recognise the accent, and I just stood there staring
while Rach giggled behind my back. Putting one of the
black straps back on my shoulder, I looked at her and said,
You try, then.

Rachel was just about to go all Spanish on us, when suddenly Sideburns' eyes illuminated and he asked, Are you
from England?

Yeah, I went, grinning my white squares. You having a
good night, then?

Yeah, I was here last night too, he said, but he didn't need
to show off. Whereabouts in England are you from?

Middlesbrough; you know, up north, I said, although I
wasn't really that interested in him. His nose was too angu-
lar and bobbly, and he seemed a bit of a ponce with his
fancy cocktails and Marlboro Lights. All his luck ended
with the cigarettes.

Oh right, I've heard it's pretty dodgy.

Ah, it's okay, Debbie said, touching her rock-hard hair.

Finishing off his bevvy, Sideburns nodded then knocked
a pair of sunglasses onto that nose. Me and Debbie laughed,
then composed ourselves when he asked us, Would you like
a drink, ladies?

What a dreamboat. I cringed then burst out laughing and
went, Naw you're alright. I thought about Mam back at the
hotel – how bad would it be if I came home spewing my

guts up. We promised her we'd go window-shopping in town tomorrow afternoon, and then some tea at the fancy place on the seafront and all of that. I didn't want to be the one who wrecked her last ever holiday. Sideburns looked at us then stumbled on a chair as he tried to get closer, and we all just shook our heads then got the hystericals as we backed away from him. I guessed we'd had enough to drink anyway.

So have you got the time then? I asked, as we started to head off.

It's four fifteen, Sideburns said, and that was the last we saw of him and the facial hair. I wasn't sure if he was fibbing, but soon the tiredness started to gang up on us and we moped around getting exceedingly bored. Drink is the crappiest drug of all – it's got potential to get you sad or violent, and you almost always end up needing a sit down. Ecstasy, on the other hand, is a big pink hovercraft you can float around on til the break of dawn. In time with the salsa drums and people's voices, we decided to step inside again but I was wondering when the night was going to end. Me, Rachel and Debbie had another dance by the podiums for the sake of it, weaving in and out of skinny brunettes and greasy hunks – me and Rach felt pretty special being the only blondies in there. The music was blaring really loud and you couldn't tell who was English or not, but we weren't that fussed about boys anyway. Soaking up the synthy strings, I tried my best to stay awake but eventually we decided to make our way back home since we were all too pooped. I could feel myself getting sober as we walked along the shiny pavements with Pacha still glowing behind us, but we were still having fun and my belly felt fine. We were already dead late, but we took our time strolling on the promenade and I guessed Mam would be asleep in any case. I really hoped she was having an alright time, even though she spent a lot of it on her own and the cancer must be always on her mind. I was just trying to block it out, but often drink triggers bad feelings and you get a bit sniffy now and then.

I clung on to my friends. As we walked, the stars, yachts and hotels all shone together in a messy white blur across Palma, and it was a really beautiful sight. I grabbed Debbie and Rachel's arms and we clicked our heels between gangs of happy foreigners, all drunk and moist as morning started to break over the Mediterranean. It must've been past five when we reached the Blue Coast Hotel, and I could feel my head dropping because I was so hot and wrecked. We took the lift up to floor four then sat on the terrace for a while, watching daylight spread across the water as we sat alone on the white plastic chairs. It would've been nice to get off with a Majorcan boy, in the hope of getting married and never having to see a grey sky again, although I couldn't just force myself on someone I wasn't even sure of. I guessed boys were all the same the world over, but I still wanted one.

Adam

Come Wednesday Abi was seeing the Prick. It was Burny and Donna's idea to go down the Viking during half-term, and I felt like a total gooseberry sat there with those four. Fucking stupid couples, I hated them. Abi was making a point of licking the Prick's face off, and I was making a point of not looking at them. We might've made a good couple, but she was weird. Abi always went on about Eve being a slag, when it was her getting her flaps out all the time. I was making a heroic effort to get pissed – I wasn't depressed but I missed Eve. It was dead boring without her, and I hated the thought of other lads getting their hands on her and me just sitting around all on my lonesome. Abi and the Prick were annoying as fuck, snogging and grinning all the time like their lips were each other's favourite penny chews. They made my skin crawl, but I had far bigger things to think about. That weekend my dad's records told me all you need is love and wouldn't you love somebody to love, and I had to admit they had a point. The songs slotted in my head like that kids' game with the hexagon and the circle and square and triangle and the holes.

'Can you pass us that?' the Prick said, picking the Richmond off Abi. It was no surprise she got him smoking as soon as they started going out, but the Prick was acting like the ladies' man and like he'd been smoking all his life. I hoped they all got lung diseases and died terrible deaths.

'You want one?' Burny went to me, holding out a Regal. It was like the pint glasses were stood in a fog of dry ice, but I'd rather be alone on a misty moor any day of the week. I shook my head, trying not to get all their crap in my eyes – I'd had it with smoking, after all I'd never seen Eve do it and I pretty much revolved around her since Rachel's party. I couldn't wait to catch her in full consciousness.

'You alright, hun?' Donna asked, but I didn't know if I was or wasn't. Most people were applying to St Mary's College after Brackenhoe, but I couldn't help thinking time was running out with Eve, or at least it was fucking dragging. Donna flashed her eyelashes at me – she had on this shiny white dress thing, but I hardly even noticed her boobs wibbling around in it. It wasn't so much that I'd lost my sex drive, I just felt a bit maturer than back in the *Razzle* days.

In fact I'd been getting on a lot better with my dad – he was finally out of the coma, his skull all bandaged but unfortunately he didn't have amnesia. I was surprised he hadn't brought up the attack though – I couldn't remember if there were stars circling his head when I smashed him with the guitar, but it was pretty serious. Perhaps he had more respect for me, now I was standing up for myself all the time – he'd started asking me about school and football and girls and this and that. I didn't bother bringing up Abi's cunt though. I didn't want to go out with her; the worst thing about not shagging Abi that night was perhaps not knowing what to do when it came to Eve.

'How long we stopping here for?' Abi asked, though it wasn't even nine yet and the pub was still filling up. Burny and Donna glanced at each other, whispered something then just shrugged and drank their drinks. We took it in turns to go to the bar, and it wasn't long before Abi and Donna got giddy and started rambling about boys. Abi was throwing her voice just to wind me up.

'So you on the Pill or what?' she asked Donna, and they both gazed at each other with criss-crossed eyes. Burny had a really big tolerance for drink, and was pretty embarrassed and all. The Prick was just a beaming smile on the end of the wet table.

'Yeah,' Donna went, scratching her arm just under the elbow.

'You still use rubbers and that?' Abi asked. 'I hate them . . .'

'Yeah, we usually stick one on.'

'Oh right, yeah, well I guess it's best to be safe not sorry, but there's nothing like him going in bareback. Proper mint orgasms all round.'

On purpose Abi flicked her eyes at me then, but I didn't even know what bareback was so it didn't matter to me. For some reason I had the image of Abi and Prickless riding ponies round an orchard together. I didn't give a fuck – they could do whatever they wanted. I started swallowing the Carling a bit quicker, waiting for my head to get melty and just block them out altogether.

'So how often youse have sex now?' Abi said next, and I rolled an eyeball. Everyone's a show-off. There had to be a lot more to life than sex – I felt sorry for those people who go out with someone they're not even sure of, just to get their end away and act all big and stuff but not even get any real joy out of them. I wanted Eve like nothing else – just sitting by her bed and making sure she was okay was the biggest rush of all. Better than skydiving and better even than Keith Richards' solo in 'The Last Time'. I just hoped it wasn't the last time I'd ever see her. I sat back and downed the rest of the Carling, wishing she'd walk through the door and I could tell her all of that. I was sick of people sleazing around girls and trying to grab them and then now and then getting their tongues down their throats and putting their dicks in them and then not really being bothered about seeing them again and maybe making them cry. If Eve heard all that, I hoped it'd make her smile – she had a big pink love-heart in the middle of her chest. Abi was wrong – she wasn't the type to go sleeping around. But I hardly saw enough of her, and I almost had a few wobbly tears going as I got up from the table. It was a bit of a lonely stupid night.

I made a trail across the patterned carpet, setting my eyes on the bar rather than the table and Abi and every-one. She was probably still talking about men's penises and women's vaginas – or probably not, seeing as I wasn't sat there. Even though I sort of shunned Abi on Sunday, I stood there and promised never to be horrible to a girl in my whole life. I tippy-tapped my fingers on the bar, ordered another Carling, then tried to compose myself a while. There was a whole host of bald and beardy drunks stood along the wood panel, and I stood there watching in the mirrors until Abi and the Prick got up for the loo. I couldn't hack it with those two any more. It's funny how you grow apart from your friends, but you still want to keep seeing them. Burny and Donna were okay, but they had the tendency to be stony silent like it was so cool to be boring. I went back to sit in the corner with them, but we couldn't really talk at all. I was a freak as well, only wanting to wallow and obsess over Eve and other various things. I wondered how she felt about me – we'd danced and she said I was sweet and we did have eye-contact now and then. God, did I really have a chance with her? My brain was a loopy tumble-drier.

'What's up with you?' Donna asked, looking over. She crossed her legs, and as if by magic she added, 'Is it girls or something?'

I nodded, but I wasn't sure how much I wanted to talk about it. I knew Donna was tiddly, and I didn't want her finding out about Abi or that I was a virgin or anything like that. She was knocking back vodkas and Cokes and she went, 'Who do you love?'

'It's just . . . Eve really,' I replied, but there wasn't much Donna could say. All of a sudden I felt embarrassed – I wasn't all that drunk, and I wondered why I thought I had a chance with her. There were a ton of nicer, hotter normal boys in school, and we'd hardly even spoken to each other. I slumped.

'She's a bit wild for you, isn't she,' Donna went, and I wondered what she was getting at.

'What are you getting at?' I asked. Eve was a nice girl compared to Abi Ellis, and I wasn't exactly a hermit any more. I started taking bigger gulps of the lager just to illustrate my point.

'Well she's on drugs, isn't she. Jenni Farrell reckons they nail pills and everything every weekend – she's a nutter. She nails a load of boys too, so I've heard. She'd eat you alive, hun.'

And that's when my heart shrunk to the size of a Smartie, and it could hardly pump my blood round and I got awful light-headed. In fact I felt like utter shit. A raincloud wandered on top of my head, and I sat back in the chair thumbing condensation off the glass. I'm not sure how much of me actually thought I'd end up going out with Eve, but sooner or later I had to wake up. Drugs scared me; the only aspect of psychedelia that excited me was all the bright clothing, and even so I was sat in the Viking wearing a grey top and boring jeans.

'I'm just off to the boys' room,' I said, getting up. The pub seemed a bit twisty as I weaved round the walls to the toilet, but it wasn't some druggy hallucination. It was me getting pissed on about three watered-down pints. What a knob I was.

In the bathroom I ran the hot tap, but it kept clicking off and I couldn't get my face splashed. I was sweating as I stood alone in the loo, my Adidases soaked a bit in piss but there wasn't much use crying over that. I'd blown it with

Eve – Abi was right about all the shagging, and all I knew about ecstasy was that episode of *Dawson's Creek* where the mental one goes off her head. Apparently all you do is say you love everyone and then collapse and go to hospital. But I didn't love anyone really, in fact I was starting to hate being in anyone's company at all. I was quite sick of myself and all.

'Ooh ooh ooh,' said the toilet door. It was a female voice, and at first I thought I was hearing things, but the cubicle carried on moaning in an orgasmic manner and I straightened up. There was a bloke's grunt there too, and it was pretty obvious what the cubicle was doing. I snuck into the stall next door – it was quite raunchy hearing two people shag, especially in public on a Wednesday evening. I adjusted my boxers, then clambered on top of the shut toilet-seat and peeped over. It was safe to say I was a weird cunt – I hadn't matured at all really. I stared over the rim. Of all the people in the world, it was Abigail and the Prick banging each other to bits in the disinfected cubicle, and my brain fucking exploded and exploded. A couple of tears popped out, and I slid back on the white cover feeling all deflated. In actual fact I was a burst red balloon. It was all too much – I wasn't man enough for Eve or Abi, and I banged my forehead off the graffiti wall cursing myself. Here's my advice to you – if you ever get the chance to lose your virginity, you should grab it. Abi was fantastic, and I threw her out. Eve was a sunbeam, but miles too hot to handle. I didn't want to be always shying away from things, and I had to slam the toilet door in my head seven times or else I'd never learn my lesson. But then it clicked – if someone else is going to love you, you've at least got to love yourself. So I pulled myself together, and as I walked out of the lav I let the door shut itself behind me. And I opened up my eyes.

Eve

Mam collapsed in the hotel bathroom in the morning, and we didn't even know about it. The chlorine water drained off my body as I pulled myself out of the swimming pool, and I stepped into a gaudy green towel then walked along the hotel terrace to the burning sun-loungers. Drying my hair, I sat between Debbie and Rachel, then looked across the harbour and wondered where Sugar Buns was. Sugar Buns was this lad I met on the beach a few days earlier, a sexy thing with daisy yellow hair and a posh-cunt accent. He was from Brighton or somewhere and his name was Justin but I much preferred to call him Sugar Buns. His arse was juicy peach jelly. Often on the sand he'd come over and try to chat us up, gobbing on about his money and his yacht and his villa up in the goldy hills, but he wasn't a complete cock. In fact he was pretty sweet, well mannered, and tanned like a cup of tea. We ended up going to his villa a couple of times for a banquet and a mess on, and I got off with him in his bedroom the first night. It was a palace. His mam and dad were okay even though they came across as a bit stuck-up, but Mam found something to chat to them about while the rest of us got stuck into sausages and stuff. We weren't yet boyfriend and girlfriend, but Sugar Buns was really nice and cute, and I had that snap-crackle-and-pop feeling in my tummy over him.

All dry, I took the lotion off Rachel then happily worked the cream around my brown bits, making sure to put tons of factor 10 on the burnt shoulders – they looked well done or at least medium rare. I rolled over on the sun-bed and unbuckled my white bikini top, reading a bit of *Mixmag* while we baked. I wasn't interested in extreme bronzing like Debbie and Rachel, who were topless and getting all the men's wandering eyes – I was more interested in little boys. Sugar Buns was sixteen, and we were texting each other non-stop, him always offering to take me for dinner at some smart restaurant or other. It was a toss-up that night between tapas or BCMs with the girls – strangely Sugar Buns wasn't game for getting pissed, but I did want to see him.

So what you gonna do? Debbie asked. Her sun-lounger was completely tarred now with graffiti.

Dunno, I'm trying to get him to come to Magaluf, but he's not into it, I replied, chucking the magazine on the bone-dry tiles. He's a bit of a saddo.

That was the problem with Sugar Buns – he had an amazing body, but he never did anything amazing with it. He preferred to stay in all the time, up in the sunny mountains like a fluorescent recluse, and he was obviously a mammy's boy. I felt it my aim to get him to live a little, get him hooked on a drug, make him a racehorse in bed, but we only had a week really and I wondered if I could be fussed.

I felt my shoulders flaring up again, so I re-hooked my bikini and had to sit under the umbrella, staring over the balcony. You could just about spot the famous cathedral in the distance, and I wondered if Sugar Buns was seeing it too.

So what you gonna do about him when you get home? Still gonna see him? Rachel asked, peeling some sunburn off her shin. I wished she didn't put it so blunt, but me and Sugar Arse had been talking about it and I said, I dunno.

He's great and that, but still not sure if it's worth all the effort. I mean we were talking about meeting in London now and then, if he really wants to make a go of it. But it's just money isn't it.

Rachel nodded, clenching all her hair together then tying it in a ponytail with these pink bands we had. She took a long swig of Evian, then passed the bottle to Deb while I played with my necklace, hoping it wasn't making a white line round my neck. I squinted in the bright lights, then laid down on the sun-sofa again and sighed. Palma was gorgeous, all stretched out beneath us with boat-masts sticking up from the sea, and I liked watching kids cycle and roller-blade while the heavy traffic shot past. Coughing, Debbie had more warm Evian then handed it to me and said, Well just see what happens. At least he's not Fairhurst anyway.

You what? I said. Since we got to Majorca the sun had sort of taken his place in my head. I felt my skin stick to the plastic bed, perching up on one elbow as I finished off the bottle.

Oh nothing, it's just you must remember Rachel's party.

Well naw, I went, feeling my belly. All it made me think of was White Lightning and achey bits and worry.

Well you know he's on smack now, don't you?

Eh? I said. I felt the cogs shift in my skull, and I tried to look out across the harbour but it was completely blinding.

Yeah, Brandon reckons so, Debbie went on, biting a fancy nail. I think he's getting it from Pullman down Grangetown. Dunno what's up with him. They just sit round people's houses not talking and being boring – Brandy reckons it started when they were snorting brown to come off Es and that. Fairhurst done twelve in one night, fucking scruff. So you probably won't be seeing much of him now anyway.

I felt my face redden and begin sizzling, and it was all such a shock I actually had to laugh. I tugged my knicker elastic then went, God, to think I wanted to get back with him at Rachel's.

Really? Rach asked. You were better off with that Adam lad.

Excuse me? I raised a drippy eyebrow. I wasn't expecting to hear that name in the middle of Majorca. I went, What's he got to do with it?

Well, you know, he took care of you while you were poorly. Kept an eye on you so you were alright. He was dead nice to you, Rachel smiled, popping on her white sixties shades.

He loves you, Debbie added, and all of a sudden a flock of tropical birds swept across the sun or at least I imagined it.

Aww, was all I could say, sighing through the warm air. I watched the little boats bob and twinkle in the water, and the whole town shivered as I blinked in the scorch. Scratching my chipped strawberry nails, I rested my head against the sun-lounger and felt my heart thump for a bit. I smiled but I was feeling funny. My tummy rumbled – I wondered if Sydney loved me too inside me. I'd definitely love her. And get her a good daddy.